The Barbershop Showdown

Canine Confidential
Book 1

Ellie Webster

Liquid Mind Publishing
This is a work of fiction. All characters, names, places and events are the product of the author's imagination or used fictitiously.

Canine Confidential Series

The Barbershop Showdown

Old Tricks, New Trouble

Chapter 1

A Clever Doggie

I took a sip of apple-cinnamon tea and pulled a face. Why did it always smell better than it tasted? Because it wasn't coffee, a little voice in my head whispered, but I ignored it.

"Mm...yum," I said to Echo, my German Shepherd, who was snoozing in his usual position on the floor beside the front counter. A beam of autumn afternoon sunlight had settled over his face and, like any senior citizen napping in the sun, he looked positively peaceful.

At nine years old, Echo wasn't showing many grays, although his stiff joints in the morning gave away his age. His medium-length coat was more black than tan. His face, head, and body were a glossy shade of midnight, while his legs and underbelly looked like he'd been dunked in a vat of coffee and cream. Just under his right eye was my favorite of his features: a faint freckling of caramel, like someone had flicked the last paint off their brush and onto his fur.

He didn't look up, so I took another sip and opened the *Cedar Hollow Crier* that lay folded on the counter in front of me. It wasn't a bad paper—two reporters, one overworked copy editor, and a part-time photographer who moonlighted at weddings—but it wasn't *The Boston Globe*.

I'd given fifteen years of my life to the *Globe*. Started there at twenty-three, fresh out of journalism school with a second-hand laptop and more opinions than experience. By the time I walked out at thirty-eight, I'd traded late-night coffee runs and breaking-news adrenaline for burnout, anti-anxiety meds, and a box of old press passes.

Sighing, I opened the *Crier* and skimmed the front page. The new golf estate on the outskirts of town was hosting a prestigious tournament. The selectboard was still dead-locked over the Main Street resurfacing budget. And, at the bottom, a photograph of last night's rare harvest moon glowing orange above the church spire. The picture was slightly out of focus, but charming. You could almost smell the woodsmoke in the air.

A pang hit me in the gut. I'd be lying if I said I didn't miss the hustle and bustle of the newsroom. The thrill of a breaking story, the research, questioning witnesses, racing against deadlines, the quest for the truth. Journalism was in my blood and walking away had been the hardest thing I'd ever done.

But Cedar Hollow was growing on me. The people were friendly, the autumn trees were gorgeous, and the Wi-Fi worked at least half of the time, even if it crawled at a snail's pace the other half.

Originally, I'd thought we'd be here three months, tops.

Long enough to fix up the store and sell it. Somehow, we hadn't left yet. The relaxed pace seemed to suit both of us.

I looked down at the paper and caught a glimpse of a tall, lean, silver-haired man congratulating a baseball player on their latest win and immediately stiffened.

Senator Graham Halstead.

He was the reason I'd quit—or close enough. The paper had slapped a gag order on a story I was about to run about his son, a Harvard senior and captain of the rowing team, who'd killed an innocent woman in a drunk-driving crash.

But that wasn't all. I might've let the article go, given the kid a break, if it hadn't been for the cover-up. The falsified report. The blood test that came back clean when I'd seen the student stumble out of the car, unable to walk straight. The officer who swore there'd been a mix-up, then stopped taking my calls.

After that, it wasn't the story that broke me. It was the moment I realized how easy it was for the truth to be buried, if the powers-that-be decide that's the way it was going to be. They made the rules, and there was nothing we could do about it.

That was not what I signed up for.

Glaring at the senator's image, I flipped the newspaper closed in disgust and walked over to the dog corner, a happy, new edition to my General Store. The sign out front still read *Cal's General Store*, and I'd left it that way out of respect for my grandfather. His gift couldn't have come at a more opportune time.

I'd spent the better part of the morning arranging a display of chew toys, tug ropes, collars, leashes, kibble, treat pouches, and scented doggy bags. There was a corkboard for lost pet posters and adoption ads, and a cushy stack of dog beds and blankets. Now, the section of my general store dedicated to all things canine was fully stocked and ready for four-legged customers.

"Whaddya think, old man?" I asked Echo. "Want to test out the new squeaky toys?"

Echo didn't flicker an eyelid. No surprise, since he was almost completely deaf. I had adopted him in the spring, before I'd moved out here to Cedar Hollow, and learning to communicate with each other had come with a steep learning curve.

"Adopted" was probably the wrong word. It wasn't like I'd been visiting animal shelters and planning for a new pet when Echo came along. More like the Boston Police Department had reached out and asked if I could provide a quiet retirement home for a newly deaf police dog with possible PTSD.

I'd been a thorn in Boston PD's side plenty of times, including when I turned up uninvited to a drug bust gone wrong and witnessed the explosion that had robbed Echo of his hearing.

It was a case of wrong place, right time. I'd been close enough to watch Echo's handler, Officer Torres, get thrown against a cement wall and Echo buried under a pile of rubble. With Torres unconscious, I'd been the one to pull Echo out and drag them both to safety.

So the cops knew me, and they knew I knew Echo. An experience like that changes a person, and I couldn't forget the brave dog I'd pulled from the rubble. I'd find myself driving past the precinct, wondering how his recovery was going. When Torres transferred to a desk job, and every other option for Echo dried up, the department had asked me to take him. For whatever reason—work-induced insanity, probably—I had said yes.

The bell above the shop door jangled. I looked up to see

broad-shouldered and burly Barry Cavanaugh step into the store. Known to everyone as "Blade," he was the town's longtime barber. His shop, Blade's Barbershop, was a few doors down from mine on the other side of Main Street.

Blade was a big guy somewhere in his 50s, with black, slicked-back hair and a permanent scowl. His shop was done up in an opulent "speakeasy" style—black leather barber's chairs, mahogany finishes, and gilded art deco fittings—and he was known for his skill with a straight razor. The man rarely came into my store; this might have been his third visit in the history of my owning the place.

"Lucy." He nodded my way.

"Can I help you with anything?" I asked brightly.

"No," Blade grumbled. He glanced around the store, then strode around me toward the cleaning supplies. Some customers just wanted to be left alone to browse. I was happy to oblige.

"Okay," I said. "I'll be here if you need me."

I piled the empty merchandise boxes behind the counter in a loose stack, then doubled back to grab a packet of Yummy Nummy dog treats, peanut butter flavor.

Ripping open the packet, I emptied the bone-shaped dog biscuits into a small bowl, then set it by the till. I was hoping to welcome lots of canine customers to The Dog's Corner, and I'd never met a furry friend willing to turn down a free treat.

That included Echo. He had settled back to sleep, the smooth black fur along his ribcage slowly rising and falling with each heavy breath. He looked peaceful, but I'd bet my life he was silently tracking my every move. Careful not to nudge him with my foot, I leaned over and dropped a treat into one of the empty boxes.

"Echo."

I reached down and lightly touched him on the back of his neck. Since he couldn't hear me, Echo and I relied on hand signals to communicate. He had been impeccably trained by Officer Torres, and I'd spent many long hours between customers trying to figure out everything he knew.

So far, that was over 15 commands. I had a feeling I'd still only scratched the surface.

Echo looked up at me with his golden-brown eyes, his black brows furrowed. He was ready to work. I'd learned pretty quickly that Echo wasn't the kind of dog who was happy to get a cookie just for being cute. This former K9 needed a job. And if I wanted to keep him from being bored out of his mind in retirement, it was *my* job to find ways to keep him employed.

I held out my hand, palm facing him, fingers angled down.

"Stand."

Echo stood, his gaze laser-focused on mine. Even though he couldn't hear me, I still said each command out loud. Cedar Hollow was a small, safe town, but I wasn't sure I wanted anyone to know he was deaf—or a highly trained former police dog. Some of the criminals Echo had busted were back on the streets after time served. If no one knew who Echo used to be—or what his weaknesses were—then he was safe.

I pointed straight at my dog, and then over at the empty boxes. "Search."

With a swish of his tail, Echo whirled around and got to work sniffling the pile of cardboard. After a few seconds, he sat down and looked at me, signaling he had found something.

"Good boy!" I cheered. I waved my hands and wiggled my fingers. Echo wagged his tail and stepped aside to let me retrieve the treat. I tossed it to him, and he caught it with a sharp snap.

"Look at that. What a clever doggy!"

I looked up to see Myrtle Trask, cheerful as usual, pushing open the shop door with her daisy-patterned shopping bag over one arm. Myrtle was a retired high school librarian, and she looked the part. Gray hair shot through with silver wisped around her ears, cozy scarf tucked into a long, wool coat, and reading glasses resting most of the way down her nose. On her collar she wore a little red-and-gold lapel pin in the shape of a book. I knew she'd given one to each of the members of her book club, the Cedar Hollow Readers' Circle, because I'd seen them wearing them when they came into the store.

"Lucy, The Boss has been at it again," she announced with a twinkle in her eye. Myrtle loved to gossip, and for some reason, she'd picked me as her favorite co-conspirator.

"The Boss" was the townspeople's affectionate nickname for Reverend Tom Heller over at First Light Chapel, thanks to his enthusiastic love of Bruce Springsteen. "Angie Muller stopped by with the flowers for Sunday's service and caught him singing *Born in the U.S.A.* from the pulpit."

I chuckled. The man was a superfan.

"Cookies!" Myrtle exclaimed in delight, spotting the dog treats by the till. She reached into the bowl. "Don't mind if I do."

"No!" I lurched across the counter and knocked her hand away. Myrtle gasped. Echo frowned up at me as if to say, *Calm down, lady.*

I winced. "I'm sorry. Those are dog treats."

"Oh! But they smell so good! Peanut butter and apple cinnamon?"

"That's my tea." I gestured to my now-lukewarm mug.

"A vendor dropped by with some new herbal teas last week, and I'm trying a new flavor every day to—"

"I know," she cut me off with a wink. "To find your new favorite, now that you've given up coffee."

I was pretty sure I hadn't told Myrtle that particular piece of information. Then again, in the six months I'd been here, I'd learned that in a small town like Cedar Hollow news travelled fast. Even news about tea, apparently.

From the back of the store, Blade dropped a bucket, and he swore as it clattered loudly against the linoleum floor.

"Oh my, *someone* woke up on the wrong side of the bed," Myrtle remarked. "Again." Her voice dropped a few tones, and she leaned forward over the counter. "His father had a hot temper, too, back when he was a parent at the school. Kept to himself, like Blade does. I heard the family has *underworld* connections, if you know what I mean."

"Really?" My reporter's ears pricked up. I hoped Blade couldn't hear her. He had obviously been in a bad mood when he walked in, and hearing Myrtle imply that his family had criminal ties probably wouldn't help. But if Blade overheard her, he didn't let on.

"Yes, there was talk—" She broke off as the doorbell jangled again, and Echo lifted his head. This time, Troy "Tank" Delgado's muscular form filled the doorframe.

Uh-oh.

An uneasy feeling gnawed at me. Those instincts were hard to put down, but it was no secret Tank and Blade were not on the best of terms. Even I knew that. Archrivals would be a better way of putting it.

Like me, Tank was a new business owner in town. He ran his own barbershop, Straight Edge Cuts, in a block of stores across town. If Blade's style was 1920s gangster, Tank's was the modern edition. Classic bad-boy, but with a meticulously clean edge. He wore his hair in a fade that tapered down from a handful of slicked-back, dark brown waves. He had two full sleeves of tattoos that he liked to show off by rolling up his sleeves, and his shirts and trousers were always sharply pressed. Tank was the kind of guy who would take you out on his motorcycle, but only if your clothes were spotless.

Echo and I weren't the only ones who clocked Tank's arrival. From across the store, Blade exploded.

"You think you can take my client?" he bellowed, striding over.

The two men met chest-to-chest in the middle of the shop floor. Myrtle gasped and clutched the countertop. Echo was immediately up and at my side, staring hard at the arguing men. Although he couldn't hear them, he sensed the animosity radiating across the store. I rested a hand on his collar.

"Everything okay?" I called, but they both ignored me, so focused were they on each other.

"You stole Bennison off my books," Blade roared, his face blistering red.

I'd heard that name before.

"The owner of the swanky Cedar Ridge Golf Estate," Myrtle stage-whispered.

I gave a nod of recognition. That was it. I'd heard his name mentioned around town.

Tank smirked as he stared Blade down.

"Aw, someone's cranky," he jeered. I could practically see steam coming out of Blade's ears. Any moment now and they were going to start throwing punches.

"You threaten my business, you threaten me," Blade barked, jabbing his finger in Tank's chest. Tank didn't flinch.

"You better back off, old man, before you get yourself hurt."

Just as I was contemplating getting Echo to break them up, Will Mercer strode in. I sighed in relief.

"Oh, thank goodness," Myrtle murmured. "Will's here."

Indeed, Will was making his presence known. The local carpenter, who had helped me renovate Cal's General when I first arrived, Will was one of the nicest, calmest guys I'd ever met.

Without hesitating, he stepped over to the two men and put a hand on Blade's shoulder.

"Why don't we get some air?" he suggested firmly. Will's voice seemed to snap Blade out of his rage. He took a half step back. Tank stayed put, a smirk on his face.

"My appointment is in twenty minutes," Will added. "What do you say we start early? I've got some lumber to pick up before five."

"Fine," Blade growled. He turned on his heel, walked over to where I was standing at the till, and tossed the cleaning supplies he'd gathered on the counter to pay. Will glanced at me over Blade's shoulder, concern in his brown eyes.

"Hey, Lucy," he said. "How are you?"

You okay?

I nodded. "Good, thanks."

I'll be fine. Thank you.

Still bristling, but exercising remarkable self-restraint, Blade grabbed his belongings and his receipt, and he and Will walked out together. Tank shot them a parting sneer, but Blade ignored him.

"Well, *that* was interesting," murmured Myrtle, recovering enough to waggle her eyebrows.

I looked down at Echo. He was staring back at me,

waiting for orders. My heart was beating triple time, which he could probably sense.

"Down," I said, then I gave him the hand signal.

Echo did as he was told and settled at my feet, but his alert gaze shifted to Tank, now browsing the snack aisle. Mine went out the glass-paneled front door to Will and Blade, still visible as they crossed Main Street and headed down the block in the fading afternoon light.

I breathed a sigh of relief. What a start to the day.

Chapter 2

Option B

Echo

I was on guard duty.

It was an hour past sundown. My human partner did her last rounds of the store where we worked the day shift, shutting off lights and switching on the security system. I stood by the door as usual, watching through the glass for any shapes moving in the dark.

My partner's job was the store.

My job was her.

In a few minutes she would step outside and lock up, and I would escort her to her car. From there, we would set off to the home we shared. She'd cook dinner and curl up with a book or a movie. I'd enjoy a can of meaty gravy over my favorite kibble and start the night shift from my fluffy bed next to the TV.

It had taken me awhile to get the hang of this new job. I'd been a cop most of my life. Thanks to my training at the academy with my first partner, Torres, I'd been a top K9 officer. Until some lowlife cooking drugs opened fire and blew up the building.

That explosion took my hearing and sent me into early retirement. Or so I'd thought. I guess the powers that be decided this old dog still had a few more tricks in him after all. Instead of putting me out to pasture, they sent me to her.

I checked on my partner over my shoulder. We were closing up later than usual. Two men had almost started a fight in the store today, and it spooked her. She'd spent an extra hour cleaning after closing time. It seemed to calm her down.

She was average height for an adult human female, and relatively fit. Her eating habits were decent: meat, cheese, vegetables, soup in cold weather, lots of sandwiches for lunch. Pasta. I could take it or leave it. Chocolate most evenings, but she didn't share. Ice cream sometimes, but not enough. She usually tossed me the end of the cone, with a good glob still at the bottom.

Her hair was the golden color of a retriever or a pointer, with no patches or stripes. It grew just past her shoulders, long enough to tickle my ears when she bent down to put on my leash. She had bright, light-colored eyes, like a husky.

She finished up entering the security code on the panel and looked at me.

"Echo."

I couldn't hear her. The sound was muffled and faint, like it came from underwater a mile away. But I could read the shape of her mouth. She knew my name, although I didn't know hers. I'd lost my hearing before we could be properly introduced.

She flicked her hand to the right.

Step to the side.

I did. She walked past me to the door and opened it. Stepped through. Patted her leg.

Come.

I followed her through the door and took my position at the back of her legs, seated against her calves, facing out into the street. Scanning for threats.

Since I didn't know her name, I'd decided to call her Rabbit. She reminded me of one. Bright, quick, and alert. Not a bad runner when we hit the trails. Cuddly when she wanted to be. And when I'd first met her, she'd been a little twitchy.

Back then, I'd just got out of the hospital. Twelve weeks all bandaged up and in a cone. I was still learning to cope without my hearing. Torres had quit the department. He'd come to see me before he transferred out. Even though I couldn't hear the words he'd said, I could tell by the tears in his eyes that it was goodbye.

My captain brought me home the day I was discharged. Then she showed up. Friendly. Heavy handed with the treats. Stressed out. Drank too much coffee. It made her jumpy.

She seemed to know me already, but I didn't remember her. Her scent, though. It seemed familiar. Then, when she took me home to start my new job, I put it all together. The explosion I'd survived had left smoke and grit up my nose for weeks afterward. I could smell traces of it on the backseat of her car, mixed with my own scent.

She'd been there. With me.

Memories flooded back. Heat, burning dust, blackness. Fingers digging into the rough of my neck, an arm scooped around my hindquarters. She'd pulled me out, carried me to safety. She'd saved my life.

And now I'd been assigned to protect hers.

At the time, I didn't know what she did for a living. Truth is, I still wasn't sure. She kept odd hours at first, up late at the computer. I could smell that her blood pressure was a little high. During the day, she'd go out and leave me behind. Against protocol. I persisted in escaping her apartment to keep up my surveillance. She was just as stubborn and kept hauling me back.

Me and this human were a lot alike.

I was only sure about one thing. She wasn't a cop. Smart, with good instincts, but low on street sense. Hardheaded, but not about rules. About finding things out. Digging things up. She had to be someone important, too. Why else would they assign me to be her personal security officer? At least, that's what I'd assumed the job was.

Then, after a few weeks together, we'd packed up and moved. Left the city and drove for hours. We landed here, in this small town, and she started working at the store. Painted it, tore out the insides and did it up nice and new, with the help of Carpenter Man.

I liked Carpenter Man. He smelled like fresh sawdust and cedar. I'd met a lot of bad men in my time on the force, and my instincts told me he was one of the good ones.

This town was safe. And slow. We lived in a small place together: one bedroom, living room carpet that smelled like a smoker went through a pack a day before I was born. Older kitchen and bathroom. Water damage behind a few layers of paint. A cat's litter box was in there once. Gone by the time we arrived. Our place sat on top of a bigger house, occupied by a man and his two kids. There was a shared backyard, but Rabbit and I barely used it. I didn't mind kids, generally. And these two liked me, sure. They were just a little too enthusiastic about chasing me around the yard when I wouldn't give up my stick.

Out here, 24/7 security seemed like overkill. But there had to be a reason Rabbit wanted us to move here. Witness protection, maybe? So I stayed vigilant. Everywhere she went, I made sure I was along for the ride. She joined me for fitness training in the mornings and learned a few of my commands. Slowly, I picked up on the fact that my role wasn't all security. She needed me for companionship. And odd jobs, too.

Down. Shake. Search that corner. Find that treat.

She was always losing treats. Good thing she'd quit coffee. She definitely needed more sleep.

When she had finished locking up, Rabbit turned and touched the back of my neck. She did that whenever she wanted me to look at her, so she could give me my orders. But this time, I ignored her. I'd spotted something down the street. There was a light on. A light that was never on this late.

In my line of work, details are important. Patterns, anything out of the ordinary. The barbershop on the corner closed by sundown. The windows were always dark when we left our store. Always.

Except tonight.

I gave a low whine and stood, ears up, pointing my nose down the street. Rabbit didn't get it. She touched my neck again. This time, I frowned up at her. She made a fist and tilted it from side to side. *Go to the car.*

Not this time.

I considered my options. I could stand there until she wondered what I was looking at. Or I could speed things up a little.

I chose option B.

I took off at a full gallop, crossing the street in two seconds flat. The shop was two doors down the block, on the street corner. I skidded to a stop outside.

Sniff, sniff.

Blood.

A thick, coppery smell that I recognized from my days on the Force. I barked, three short alerts.

Blood detected! Possible victim!

Rabbit caught up to me, puffing and saying *a lot* of words that only filtered through as muffled chirps. She grabbed my collar, then froze. Leaning forward, she peered through the front window of the shop. I wriggled, trying to loose myself from her grip so I could jump up and get a glimpse. She wouldn't let me. I looked up at her.

Sit, she signaled. *Sit. Sit!*

I sat.

With one finger still hooked under my collar, Rabbit fumbled in her bag and pulled out her phone. She punched in three digits. I knew what that meant. Emergency.

We waited only a few minutes before the sheriff's black-and-white pulled up, lights flashing. Good. I liked the sheriff. She didn't have a K9 officer on her team, but I didn't mind lending an assist.

Another cruiser pulled in behind, carrying two deputies. As the officers approached, Rabbit took a step back. She released my collar so I could follow. First I had to assess the scene.

Jumping up against the shop window, I looked inside. There was a body on a chair. It was still. Too still. I breathed in, snorting my nose against the glass. A faint odor reached me through a few cracks in the window seal.

Dead.

It was the man who ran the shop. The one who had been in the store today: big and burly, smelled like tobacco and hair grease. He was slumped in a chair, facing the mirror. One hand on the armrest, the other hanging limp by his side. Wound on his neck—a fresh one. Fatal. Blood pooled around the base of the chair.

Something gleamed on the floor, in the blood. A weapon. Some kind of blade. I barked twice. *Danger! Weapon on scene!*

Rabbit hauled me back to the sidewalk by my collar. I didn't blame her for being rough. She wasn't a cop; she wasn't used to blood.

And we'd just discovered a murder.

Chapter 3

Razor's Edge

That *dog* of mine.

I wrangled Echo into a "down" on the sidewalk and commanded him to stay. He blinked up at me, the flashing lights of Sheriff Annie's cruiser reflecting in his eyes. He couldn't have looked any more like a police dog if he'd been wearing a gun and a badge.

"Good thing he's cute," remarked Sheriff Annie, arriving at my side. "Did you enter the scene?" She eyeballed Echo. "Did you?"

"No, but he alerted me that something was wrong." On cue, Echo thumped his tail on the concrete.

"Good boy," the sheriff said.

I liked Sheriff Annie Rae Dalton. She was somewhere in her late fifties, her auburn hair threaded with gray. The lines on her face told of a life led by clear-headed thinking and common sense. Myrtle had told me she knew every personality in town—had babysat most of them when they were younger—and she didn't put up with bad behavior.

"What did you see?" she asked me. We both turned to look through the window of Blade's Barbershop. The proprietor, Blade, was dead on a barber's chair. His throat had been cut.

I'd be lying if I said I wasn't trembling a little from shock. I'd seen dead bodies before. Been at many a crime scene, but only after the fact.

I'd never found a murder victim before.

Only hours earlier, Blade had been in my store, full of life—and rage.

"Nothing," I admitted. "Echo dragged me over here after I closed up. Maybe he noticed the light was on. Blade usually closes before we do."

"You think he picked up on that?" Sheriff Annie asked. She glanced down at my dog. He was watching her eagerly. Probably hoping his discovery would land him a job at Cedar Hollow Sheriff's Department.

"He's a smart cookie." Like everybody else in town, Sheriff Annie didn't know Echo was a former K9 officer. My plan for Echo's safety was to keep it that way.

I spotted something glinting in the pool of blood. A straight razor, a fancy one with an ornate silver handle. It looked like it could have come from Blade's own shop.

"That razor, in the blood." I pointed through the window. "Could that be—"

"Looks like one of his," nodded Sheriff Annie. "Well spotted. I see you haven't lost your investigative eye for detail."

I smirked. It seemed news of my previous career had spread around town.

Shrugging, I didn't respond. That part of my life was over.

"I'll confirm it," she added. "You didn't see anyone come or go? Any odd activity around Blade's shop today?"

I shook my head. "I can't see into his shop from where I am." Then I remembered the obvious. "Oh, but he had a fight in my store today—with Tank Delgado."

"A fight?" Sheriff Annie looked as surprised as I'd felt when it happened.

"Argument," I amended. "Blade came in for some cleaning supplies, then Tank showed up, and Blade blew up at him. He was yelling at him for poaching a client. Harold Bennison."

"Bennison," the sheriff said, more to herself than to me. "He owns the golf course. Rich fellow. So Blade was pretty upset?"

"Furious. I thought he was going to knock Tank's head off."

"And Tank? How did he react?"

"He held his own," I said. "Made it clear that he didn't care Blade was angry. Thank God Will walked in when he did."

Sheriff Annie looked at me. "Will Mercer?"

I nodded. "He got Blade to leave. They had an appointment, but Will convinced him to start early."

"What time was this?"

"Around four, four-thirty."

"Not long before Blade would have closed for the day," Sheriff Annie remarked. She looked pensive. "I'll have to talk to both of them, then."

A silence settled between us, and I realized what the sheriff was thinking. Tank was a person of interest, obviously, since he and Blade had almost come to blows that afternoon. But Will might have been Blade's last appointment of the day. Maybe even the last person to see him alive.

No. Not Will.

There was no way Will Mercer had anything to do with Blade's murder. Calm, generous, hardworking. I'd covered a lot of crime in my career, and Will just wasn't the type.

I hope I didn't get him in trouble.

Sheriff Annie went inside the shop with one of the deputies, and the other stayed outside to guard the door. With the blue and red lights flashing off the surrounding buildings, it didn't take long for a handful of curious Cedar Hollow residents to appear. Will drove past in his red Ford pickup, but he quickly pulled over and parked down the block when he spotted Echo and me.

"Everything okay?" he asked as he approached, his brow creased with worry. Before I could answer, Myrtle appeared, puffing a little from what was probably a mad dash down the street to see what was going on.

Before the deputy could stop her, she pressed her nose to the glass and peered through the barbershop window. The rosy blush drained from her cheeks.

"My word!" she gasped. "Is that Blade? Is he... *dead?*"

"Barry's dead?" someone cried. A woman, a well-dressed brunette in her late forties, appeared from around the corner and tried to push through to the shop door. The deputy intervened, and Sheriff Annie stepped back outside.

"Is it Barry? Is he dead?" the woman demanded, her voice high and sharp. Suddenly, Sheriff Annie seemed to recognize her, and her expression softened.

"Colleen," she said gently. "I'm so sorry. Yes, Blade is dead."

The woman, Colleen, crumpled. Will and the deputy each caught one arm, and Sheriff Annie directed them to help her take a seat in the back of the police cruiser.

"My word, it *is* Colleen," Myrtle hissed. "I almost didn't recognize her!"

"Who's Colleen?" I asked.

"Blade's sister." Myrtle's eyes were round. "She moved away years ago. What awful timing, to come home just in time to find her brother killed!" Her sharp-eyed gaze shifted to me. "What happened in there? Did you see anything?"

"Myrtle, you need to let us do our job," Sheriff Annie interrupted firmly, as Will returned to our group. "Will, can I have a word?"

My stomach did a queasy flip as I watched Will oblige. He followed the sheriff, and they stepped out of earshot. Myrtle clutched my arm.

"What do you think they're talking about?" she demanded breathlessly. "Was Will already here when you got here? Was he inside the shop with Blade's body?"

Echo looked at me, then at Myrtle, then back to me, his forehead rumpled. I could practically read his thoughts.

Step away and keep your hands where I can see them.

I ignored Myrtle's questions for two reasons. One: there was no way Sheriff Annie would want me sharing crime scene details with Cedar Hollow's most notorious gossip. Two: staying on good terms with the sheriff might mean I'd get an inside look at what was going on in the investigation.

For curiosity's sake. Since I wasn't a journalist anymore.

"Colleen looks devastated," I offered instead. I pointedly looked over at the sheriff's cruiser. Blade's sister was leaning forward in the backseat, her head in her hands, body wracked with sobs. "I wonder if there's anyone in town she could talk to."

I let that notion hang in the air, hoping Myrtle would take the bait. After a few seconds, the opportunity clicked.

"She might have *a lot* to say about her brother that would shed some light on things," she murmured. "Poor thing. I'll go and make sure she gets home all right."

As Myrtle bustled over to offer Colleen a listening ear, Will and the sheriff reappeared from around the corner.

"Thanks for your time," the sheriff said to him. She nodded to her deputy, then re-entered the barbershop.

"Everything okay?" I asked hopefully. I knew the answer was probably "yes," considering Sheriff Annie hadn't swapped Colleen for Will in the back of her cruiser.

"Yup, just a few standard questions." Will looked completely calm, not worried or stressed about being considered a suspect. "You've got your car, right? Would you like me to follow you home?"

"That's okay, I'll be fine." He didn't need to know this wasn't my first time at a crime scene. Besides, I had my own security detail.

I thought I saw disappointment flicker across Will's face when I declined his offer, but I chose not to read too much into it. I looked down at Echo. He was already staring back, ready for orders.

We had moved here for a new life, a quiet one. Cedar Hollow was a safe town. A small town. I didn't know what had happened to Blade, but, for the sake of my new life here —and Echo's—I couldn't let myself think about it too much.

I patted my leg. "Come."

Echo stood, and we headed down the sidewalk to my car.

With a little luck, Sheriff Annie would probably have this tied up by Saturday.

Chapter 4

Pumpkin Vibes Just Don't Cut It

The next morning, as I breathed in the spicy aroma of my decaffeinated "Pumpkin Vibes" tea, I found myself mulling over Blade's murder. It was hard not to. I'd never expected to find a dead man in the barbershop down the street from my store. Not in this quiet, leafy town.

It was the kind of story I used to live for. A murder... unfolding in my own street. News gold.

I knew I shouldn't get involved, but the few facts I knew were swirling around in my head. It couldn't hurt to make a mental list of what I knew so far.

Someone had killed Blade Cavanaugh with his own razor. Sheriff Annie would confirm that, but for now I took it as an accurate assumption. Blade had fought with Tank

Delgado earlier in the day. Tank Delgado also owned a barbershop and according to Blade, had stolen a wealthy client off his books. The two men were business rivals.

Except their argument had seemed personal. My gut was telling me there was more to this than met the eye. And then there was poor Will caught in the middle. What bad luck he'd been Blade's last appointment on the day of the murder.

Or good luck, depending on how you looked at it. He had stepped in and saved the day when the altercation had happened in my store. I was grateful to him for that.

Was stealing a customer, even one as wealthy as Bennison, enough of a motive for murder?

I shook my head. Here I was, back in investigative reporter mode, treating this small-town murder like a big-city conspiracy.

The whole thing was probably simple. A panicked burglar, maybe. The razor belonged to Blade, so the murder might have been nothing more than a crime of opportunity —the intruder grabbing the nearest weapon at hand.

I sighed. Maybe I missed my old life more than I wanted to admit.

Looking down at Echo, I said, "Whaddya think, old man? Do you miss your old job?"

Echo was dozing in his usual spot, ready for action at a moment's notice. As usual, he didn't respond, although he did lift his head and stare through the glass-paneled door of the shop. Across the street, Myrtle was bustling down the sidewalk at speed. Knowing Myrtle, this was a sure sign she was bursting with some kind of neighborhood gossip, and on her way to find someone to share it with.

I felt a sudden desire to be in the loop.

"Break time," I told Echo, and stepped out from behind

the counter. He looked up at me, and I patted my leg. "Come."

I slapped a "Be Back in Five" sign on the door and locked up just in time to see Myrtle make her way inside The Spotted Spoon. I'd always liked the local diner. The atmosphere was warm and welcoming, and the blueberry muffins delicious. I could see why they had such a stellar reputation.

I pushed open the door and took a moment to inhale the delicious aromas of pancakes and bacon. The diner was busy as usual with morning patrons. Sheriff Annie perched at the counter with her hands wrapped around a white ceramic mug. Junebug Harris, the mailman, was seated at a table, enjoying a latte and one of the diner's famous muffins. A group of young mothers and their toddlers had spread out in the sunny corner by the front window. Myrtle had settled into a booth by the opposite window.

"Morning, Lucy!" Betty called cheerfully from behind the counter. She and her husband, Boyd, both in their 60s, had come out of retirement to run the place after it had come up for sale a few years ago, I was told. The previous owner had cooked the books and ended up in a white-collar prison—according to Myrtle.

Betty picked up a freshly brewed pot of coffee and refilled the sheriff's mug. "I've told you, dear," she added in my direction, "if you want a coffee, just give me a call and I'll have Boyd bring it over. No need to shut the store."

On cue, Betty's husband Boyd stuck his head out of the back storeroom and gave me a wave. "Yup, no trouble at all!"

"See?" said Betty. "He's happy as a clam when he can get out of doing work around here."

"Hey!" Boyd protested. "Who volunteered to clear out all these boxes today?"

"You did, dear, and I'm very grateful. Especially since I asked you to do it last spring!"

I offered a polite smile but no comment. Betty and Boyd's bickering was as much a feature of The Spotted Spoon as their blueberry muffins.

Betty bustled around the edge of the counter with the pot of coffee. As soon as she saw Echo, she frowned and flicked her hand toward the door.

"Echo, *out*. I'm sorry, Lucy, I can't have him in here after he stole that pancake off Reverend Heller's plate last week."

In Echo's defence, the reverend liked to "accidentally" drop bites of breakfast under the table. Echo cued to the wave of Betty's hand and took one precise step to the left. By pure luck, that put him directly into the path of a wayward toddler about to fall over. Just in time, the child reached out and steadied herself on Echo's back. The toddler's mom rushed over.

"What a good doggy!" she cried, swooping the child into her arms. Echo looked at Betty and thumped his tail on the floor.

"Well," Betty clucked, relenting. "I guess he can stay."

"Thanks, Betty." I smiled gratefully. "I'll keep a close eye on him."

Betty turned away just in time to miss Junebug holding out a piece of muffin for Echo. Since the mailman was known to hate every dog in Cedar Hollow except mine, I decided to turn a blind eye.

As I made my way over to Myrtle, I was very aware that Sheriff Annie was within earshot over at the diner counter.

Luckily, she checked her watch, swigged the last of her coffee, and left.

"Do you mind if I join you?" I asked Myrtle. I slid into the booth, and Echo settled on the floor next to us, his gaze still fixed on Junebug and the last few bites of his muffin.

"What's news?" I could see she was just bursting to share.

Myrtle leaned over, lowering her voice. "A little bird told me that Blade owed Will Mercer money. A *lot* of money."

My eyes widened. "For what?"

I knew Will was generous. I'd seen him offer to fix a porch or two for free if people couldn't afford the repair. But I couldn't imagine him lending out wads of cash.

"Apparently, Will did the renovation job on Blade's Barbershop, but Blade never paid him."

"How long ago did that happen?" I'd only been in Cedar Hollow for six months, and Blade's Barbershop hadn't gone through any major changes in that time.

"Let's see," Myrtle said, frowning. "It would have been last summer, I think."

My eyebrows shot up. "Blade owed Will money for over a *year?*"

"It was a big job, too," she added gleefully. "Blade's shop was under construction for months." She clicked her tongue. "I should know. I was stuck with the sound of hammers all day."

I looked at her blankly.

"I live across the street, dear," Myrtle explained. "The way I heard it, Blade kept promising to pay, but he never did. The barbershop must have been doing awfully badly."

So Blade's business had taken a nosedive before he

could pay Will for his work. Is that why his sister was visiting? Had he reached out to Colleen and asked her for money?

Myrtle fell into contented silence, sipping her coffee with the peace of a newly unburdened soul.

My mind was racing. A longstanding debt. That could be construed as a solid motive for murder.

I sat with Myrtle for a few more minutes, then said I had to get back to the store. When I stepped out of the diner, something down the street caught my eye. Will's dusty red Ford pickup was parked at the police station.

Will was being formally questioned by the sheriff.

It was almost dark when I left Cal's General, but Echo and I weren't headed home just yet. I had spent all afternoon imagining Will as a suspect in Blade's murder, but knowing his character, I just couldn't get there. I needed to talk to him.

When I had first arrived in Cedar Hollow and decided to renovate the store, Will had been recommended by every resident I spoke to. Once I'd hired him, I found out why. He was dependable, detailed, and an expert craftsman.

Will had told me he'd been a carpenter over half his life. He had started as an apprentice in his dad's shop in his teens. After leaving town for a short stint, he'd returned to look after his sister when his parents had passed. Now he ran Mercer & Sons.

He had been more than generous with his time and expertise during my renovation, and, thanks to his spotting old electrical wiring in the walls of my 50-year-old store, he had probably saved the building from burning to the ground.

It also didn't hurt that, at six feet tall, with shaggy brown hair, warm brown eyes, and a workman's muscular build, he was definitely easy on the eyes.

Just as I'd hoped, Will's pickup was back outside Mercer & Sons. His woodshop was on Main Street, but in the opposite direction of Blade's Barbershop. The light from inside beamed through the windows into the cold autumn dark, so I knew he was there.

I knocked first, then pushed open the door.

"Hello?" I called out. "I come bearing gifts."

The reception area held Will's mahogany desk, a few chairs, and a coffee station with a mini fridge. On the walls hung samples of his craftsmanship. Beveled bedposts, short lengths of staircase railing, and four cupboard doors in different styles and stains.

The second time I met Will—after his first visit to the store for a 3:00 p.m. chocolate bar pick-me-up—we'd sat here discussing ideas, quotes, and plans.

Through a wide window in the dividing wall, I could see into the workshop beyond. Stacks of timber in every shape and size lined the back wall, while three sturdy work-tables stood neatly in the center. One held a table saw, the others different types of saws whose names I couldn't begin to guess. Shelves along the side walls were crowded with carving tools, hand saws, and rows of tins filled with sealant and stain, their faint, woody scent lingering in the air.

Will looked up from his workbench, and I could see he was surprised. I held up a bag of chips. Classic salted, the kind he liked to buy at my store. Smiling, he pulled off his protective glasses and came through the shop door.

"Hi." He accepted the snack with a grin. "It's good to see you."

Before I could answer, Echo barged past Will into the

woodshop. He was in heaven, exploring every corner of the room and snuffling through the thin layer of wood dust on the concrete floor.

"Echo," I called, shooting Will an apologetic look. He waved his hand as if to say he was fine with it. Not that Echo could hear me anyway.

"Would you like a coffee?" He gestured to his hot drink setup. He'd built a custom stand with shelves for his coffee maker and canisters of coffee, sugar, sweetener, hot chocolate mix, and chamomile tea. I dug deep to find my resolve.

"Thanks," I said, "but I'm trying to quit."

"I've got decaf."

I had to admit a hot cup of Joe would really hit the spot. Without caffeine, what harm could it do?

"You've twisted my arm," I conceded. "Yes, please."

As he stepped over to the coffee maker, Echo pawed at the shop door. I let him in, and right away he spotted the work gloves dangling from Will's back pocket.

"Heads up," I warned. "Glove thief on the prowl."

"I'm ready." Will was already wise to the game. He made a big show of fussing with the machine while Echo crept closer, tail stiff, ears high. A neat tug later, and the gloves were out.

Echo dropped them proudly and barked once.

"Busted," Will said with a laugh, pretending surprise. I waved at Echo, then rewarded him with a Yummy Nummy treat.

Will shook his head, smiling. "That dog's got more personality than half the people in town."

"Smart, too," I said. "He's never wrong about people."

Will turned back to the coffee machine. I decided to broach the subject I'd come to talk about.

"I saw your truck at the police station earlier," I said, hesitantly.

"Yeah, the sheriff called me in today," he admitted.

"I'm sorry. I think that was my fault. I told her about the altercation in the store, and you taking Blade back to his barbershop." I cringed.

He shrugged. "It's not your fault. I was the last person to see him alive."

"Apart from the killer, of course," I pointed out.

He glanced at me. "Of course."

"And it doesn't help that you have a motive," I murmured.

"What?" He looked confused.

"Oh, I don't mean... I mean I don't think you..."

"What motive?" he repeated, his gaze narrowing as he handed me the mug.

I gulped, accepting it with a nod of thanks. "Myrtle told me about the money Blade owed you."

"Oh, that." He sighed, and the muscles in his jaw popped. His gaze followed Echo, who was now nosing around a two-by-four.

"I always thought you were on good terms with Blade."

"I am, or rather, I was. The money thing was getting in the way though. He kept promising to cough up, but he never did."

"I'm surprised you waited this long," I remarked.

He leaned against the wall, arms folded. "Truth is, Blade and I did get into it that night. After he cut my hair, I brought up the money. Told him I'd take him to small claims court if he didn't pay."

"Let me guess? He didn't take it well?"

"That's putting it mildly. He blew up, told me to get out. So I left."

He wasn't in the best mood yesterday to begin with. I could only imagine what effect Will's words had on him.

"And you told this to Sheriff Annie?"

"Yeah, but he was alive and kicking when I left. I promise you that much."

I didn't doubt him.

But right now there didn't seem to be many suspects, other than Tank. And Will was Blade's last appointment of the day.

"You didn't see anything strange when you left?" I asked, knowing Annie would have asked him the same thing.

He cracked a grin. "I can see you used to be a reporter."

"What? No. I mean, yeah, but—" How did he know?

"Word gets around," he said. "And I have a confession to make. I Googled you."

"You did?" I felt my eyes widening.

"Yeah. Hope you don't mind. The Boston Globe. Wow."

I felt my face growing hot.

"I'm not that person anymore," I said.

He gave me a strange look. "Why'd you leave?" he asked, after a beat.

This was something I definitely didn't want to talk about.

"Do you mind if we don't get into this now?" I said, draining my coffee.

"That bad, eh?" He was still studying me. I felt the need to get away from his scrutiny. I'd come here to ask him some questions, and instead, I was the one under the microscope. Or that's how it felt. I knew Will didn't mean any harm, and I was still sensitive about what had happened.

"Oh, it's nothing," I said, getting up and patting my leg.

Echo, who'd been lying beside me, scrambled to his feet. "I just got burned out."

He gave a knowing nod.

"Maybe someday you'll tell me the story, then?"

He was far too intuitive.

"Thanks for the coffee," I said, and will Echo on my heels, left the workshop.

Chapter 5

A Surprise Stroll

As I stretched out my hamstrings, squinting into the morning sun that streamed through the east-facing window of my store, I considered that today might be the day I get back together with caffeine.

Will made *excellent* coffee, even if it had been decaf. And the coffee cream back in Boston never tasted half as good. But the real reason for my temptation to rejoin the dark roast side? I'd been up early for my pre-dawn jog with Echo—after doing a deep dive online that lasted until 1:00 a.m. I'd been trying to figure out everything I could about Blade, his family, and who could have possibly wanted him dead.

This morning's "Ginger Snap" tea just wasn't cutting it.

I balanced myself on the counter with one hand and used the other to grab my left ankle from behind, pulling back my bent leg in a quad stretch. Now that I was in my late thirties, loosening up a few times a day was almost a requirement for mobility.

I didn't for a moment think Will had anything to do with Blade's murder. I was a pretty good judge of character, and he wasn't the murdering type. And with the number of criminals Echo had encountered during his career, I trusted my dog's judgment as much as I did my own—if not more.

Besides, Blade owed Will money. With Blade dead, Will had to swallow the loss. Why would he kill Blade if it guaranteed that he wouldn't get paid?

I was sure Sheriff Annie would reach the same conclusion herself. But it couldn't hurt to dig up a little evidence to help the investigation along. The problem was, I hadn't found anything online that would point to even the shakiest motive for murder.

I stopped stretching and stirred my tea, trying to imagine it was a chai latte with a shot of espresso. As far as I could tell, the whole "crime family" thing I'd heard from Myrtle was completely made up. Blade might have passed for a mobster, given his slicked-back hair and bad attitude, but there was nothing else I could find online to substantiate that rumor. I had searched local crime news and public court records, trying to find evidence of any criminal history. Blade had never even shoplifted a candy bar, let alone been suspected of "underworld connections." He didn't have a social media profile, either, or even a business website. It seemed like only one thing Myrtle had said was right. The man had kept to himself.

As for his and Colleen's parents, both had passed away

within the last ten years. Separately, and due to natural causes. I had learned the most about them from their obituaries. Anne and Donald Cavanaugh were "loving parents," and Anne had been a fan of jigsaw puzzles. Donald Cavanaugh, on the other hand, had been known for his deadly swing—on the golf course.

Next, I had dug into Blade's Barbershop. Blade's Barbershop had been in operation for almost 20 years, but the building had been owned by his family for a lot longer. What they'd used it for, I had no idea. The only snippet of information I found came from the *Cedar Hollow Crier*, when it had reported on the shop's restoration last year.

The site of Blade's Barbershop on the corner of Main Street and Spurlock has been owned by the Cavanaugh family since 1923. Current owner Barry Cavanaugh says that the refurbishment is a nod to the "speakeasy" style of the era.

And Colleen? She was a professor of biology at the state university—I found her listed on their website with a very professional headshot. She had a social media presence, but it was extremely pared down. Her profile picture was the same headshot used by the university, and she had about 23 friends. Her security settings prevented me from seeing who they were.

From what I could find online, Blade had run a reputable business, and his family had zero criminal connections.

So why would someone have wanted the man dead?

The golden rule in any investigation was to follow the money, but I couldn't find anything shady there, either.

Presumably Blade had taken out an insurance policy on the barbershop. Standard stuff. Customer injury, fire damage, theft. But nothing had been stolen or broken the night of the murder, and he'd been the only one hurt.

By mid-morning, I decided to give in.

"Time for a coffee," I told Echo, and patted my leg for him to follow. Six months had been a good run. I had almost given a customer $20 change for their ten-dollar-bill, and enough was enough.

I stuck my "Be Back in Five" sign on the door and headed down the street with Echo to The Spotted Spoon. Approaching the diner from the opposite direction was a middle-aged brunette I recognized from the scene of Blade's murder. It was his sister, Colleen.

"Hi," I said, pausing to wait for her to reach the door. "You're Colleen, right?"

"Yes," she said uncertainly. "And you are—?"

"Lucy. I'm the one who found your brother. I'm so sorry for your loss."

She gave a small nod. "Thank you."

"How are you?" I asked, knowing it was a stupid question. *How have you been since your brother was brutally murdered?*

"I'm doing as well as I can be." She paused, as though she were deciding whether to go inside the diner or not. In the end, she sighed, "It's been a little difficult getting through this on my own here. I haven't been back to Cedar Hollow in a long time, and I'd lost touch with almost everyone."

"That does sound tough," I sympathized.

She looked down at Echo, who was staring intently through the diner's front window. Probably narrowing down the suspect most likely to give him their leftovers.

"You have a beautiful dog," she remarked. "I've always loved shepherds. It's been a dream of mine to own one someday, when I have more time—maybe when I'm close to retirement. I've heard they require a lot of attention."

"That's definitely true of Echo, here," I laughed. "And a lot of brushing, too."

Echo looked up at me, as if to say, *Are we going in, or what?*

"I was just about to take him for a walk along the forest trail," I lied, gesturing up the street. "Would you like to join us?"

Colleen broke into a surprised smile. "Oh, I'm not dressed for walking, but that would be nice."

I eyed her tailored trousers and silk blouse. At least she was wearing flat shoes. "We won't go far."

She gave a pleased nod. "In that case... My coffee can wait."

It would have to. This was far more important.

Although the state of Vermont was famous for its beautiful trees—especially in the autumn, when the leaves turned to breathtaking shades of red, yellow, and orange—Cedar Hollow itself was known for its namesake: wide, towering cedar trees that stood in the yards, along the roads, and at streetcorners across town. A few blocks down from the center of commerce on Main Street was a belt of cedar forest that featured a winding trail popular with dog walkers, runners, and birdwatchers.

"I always loved this place," said Colleen as we stepped onto the gravel trail that led into the trees. The forest was cool and quiet, save for the occasional birdsong. I reached down to give Echo the okay to run free. He and I often jogged through here in the mornings, and he had almost flawless recall—except when a small woodland creature was involved.

Once my dog was off and sniffing, I took a deep,

relaxing breath. There was a stillness here that I had never come close to finding in Boston. From the corner of my eye, I could see the forest starting to work its magic on Colleen, too. She relaxed her shoulders, and a look of contentment came over her face.

"Barry and I used to come here all the time when we were kids," she said, gazing up at the trees.

I nodded but said nothing. I had decided to lean on an old interviewer's trick: staying quiet. Sometimes, offering a little silence prompted people to fill it.

"We loved messing around in here, you know?" Colleen said. "Making little forts, playing hide and seek." Another pause. "Things were so much simpler then. But everything is always simpler when you're a kid, right?"

I sensed it was the right time for a question. "Was Blade having trouble with anyone?" Then, so I wouldn't sound like I was interrogating her: "His death just seems so sudden. Completely out of nowhere."

"I know," Colleen agreed. "I have no idea. Truly. Barry was a grumpy old fart sometimes, but he didn't have any enemies that I knew of. We weren't as close as we used to be, but I think I'd still know if someone wanted him dead."

"Hmm," I nodded. We fell into another silence.

"The only thing I can think of," she added after a moment, "is that he told me he was about to come into some money."

My ears perked up.

"He gave me a call out of the blue last week and said we were long overdue for a visit. He suggested I come here—he said he wanted to tell me all about a private buyer he had found for the barbershop. Apparently, it was going to be a lucrative deal; the buyer was prepared to pay more than the building was worth."

Right away, something about that didn't add up. Blade wanting to sell the barbershop I could believe, especially knowing he had debts to Will that he couldn't pay. But with a buyer lined up and one foot out the door, why had he blown up at Tank for poaching his client, Harold Bennison?

"I'm just so devastated that I missed him," Colleen added, snapping me out of my speculation. "I arrived the night Barry was killed, but I never got the chance to speak with him. I stopped by the shop and said a quick hello, but I had dinner plans that night with my old friend, Parker." She shook her head sadly. "I thought I had time."

"Parker?" I prompted, not recognizing the name.

"Parker Dewey," she said. "He's one of the only people I've kept in touch with from my high school track days. His wife is lovely, too. He works as a historian now, at the Cedar Hollow Historical Society. They have an office at the library."

"Late fifties, graying hair, dapper dresser?" I'd spotted him there a few times. It was hard to forget a man wearing a waistcoat and a spotted cravat.

Colleen chuckled. "That's Parker. He's not the best at emotional conversations, but he's the only friend I still have in this town."

"Well, now you have one more," I said kindly.

She smiled appreciatively. "Thank you. This walk has been just what I needed. Maybe I can join you and Echo for another one before I go."

"Absolutely," I said. "When are you planning to head home?"

"In a few days," Colleen said. "I hope Sheriff Annie has some answers for me by then. It would really help, I think, to find out who did this to poor Barry."

"That's what we all want," I agreed. The murder had

made everyone around town uneasy. I'd heard customers talking about it in hushed tones. It didn't help that the Main Street shop was wrapped in bright yellow crime tape. "Sheriff Annie is very competent. I'm sure she'll get to the bottom of it soon."

I hoped I sounded a lot more confident than I felt.

Chapter 6

An Odd Coincidence

Back at Cal's General—without a coffee, since I had run about 30 minutes over the break I'd expected to take—I steeped another herbal tea and mulled over what I had learned.

Blade had told Colleen he was about to come into some money. That he'd found a buyer for the barbershop. Now that was interesting. I hadn't heard anything to that effect, and in this town, that was surprising. Either it was the best kept secret of the year, or it was a lie.

Yet why would he lie to Colleen?

I decided some more investigative work into that deal was in order.

There was one lead that I did have, however. And that

was something I'd witnessed with my own eyes. Blade going toe-to-toe with Tank Delgado in the middle of my store.

I'd never been to Tank's barbershop before. Maybe it was time to pay him a friendly visit—and to see if I could find out where he was the night of the murder. I wondered if Sheriff Annie had questioned him too? After what I'd told her about the altercation, I certainly hoped so.

Some rival businesses like to square off on opposite corners of the same street, like competing gas stations or pizzerias in New York City. But when Tank had opened Straight Edge Cuts, he had staked out his own patch of Cedar Hollow across town from Blade's shop. After I closed my own store at 6:30 p.m., Echo and I jumped in the car and headed over. Since it was a Friday, I was betting Tank's shop would be open late. As I rounded the corner to the mini strip of storefronts on Church Hill Road, I saw that the red, blue and white barber's pole out front was still lit and turning.

Straight Edge Cuts sat at the end of a row of four retail spaces. The block was newer than the storefronts on Main Street, but they had obviously been built to match the town's quaint aesthetic: each was red brick with a wooden awning, and the far edge of the front sidewalk was lined with flowerboxes. In the window of Tank's shop glowed a neon sign that read: "Open." Above that, an extra-large black decal of a straight razor, with "Straight Edge Cuts" underneath.

I parked outside, right next to Tank's gleaming black motorcycle. Through the shop's front window, I could see he was with a customer I recognized: "The Boss," aka Reverend Heller. I knew I'd get a warm reception from the reverend. Aside from clearly having a fondness for Echo, he was generally nice to everyone. Hopefully, The Boss would help me break the ice, and I'd get some information out of Tank.

I reached over to Echo and ruffled the thick, black fur between his ears. He had climbed into the front seat next to me and was sitting bolt upright, staring at Tank. Echo was protective of me, and Tank had been one half of an argument the last time he was in Cal's General.

"Whaddya think, old man?" I asked. "Should we wing it?"

Echo didn't answer. I took that as a yes.

When I pushed open the door to the barbershop, Tank was in the middle of expertly applying a straight razor to the foamy surface of the reverend's face and neck. Like Tank himself, the inside of his shop was clean and classic with an edge: black leather chairs sitting on stainless steel claw pedestals, a spotless black-and-white checked floor, and a white neon sign of the shop's straight razor logo hanging on the wall.

Both men looked over at me, and Tank's eyebrows shot up in surprise.

"Lucy and Echo!" Reverend Heller exclaimed, clearly delighted. He patted his leg for Echo to come over, but Echo was too busy eyeing Tank to respond.

Tank, for his part, didn't seem to mind that I was standing in his shop, but he didn't look happy to see my dog.

"Can I help you?" he asked. He pointedly eyed Echo as he started sniffing around. "He's not going to pee in here, is he?"

"No, he just went," I said brightly. "Sorry to interrupt, I was just looking for a barber. For my brother. He's visiting in a few weeks, and I wanted to check this place out before he gets here."

It wasn't a total lie. I'm sure that, if I had a brother, and he was planning to visit, he would need a haircut at some point.

Reverend Heller beamed, no doubt already ready to welcome my family to Cedar Hollow. Tank didn't look impressed.

"This is it. Any questions?"

Before I could answer, he shot another glower at Echo, who was loping past on his third tour of sniffing the floor. "Look, I'm in the middle of an appointment," he added sharply. "There's a list of services and prices online."

Bringing my dog along had been a bad move, I realized. If there was any chance Tank might have talked to me before, he definitely wasn't in a chatty mood now.

But maybe there was a way I could get a look at his appointment book. If he'd been with a client the night of Blade's murder, he couldn't have been responsible. I thought fast. "Do you have a bathroom? Sorry. It's urgent."

Clearly against his better judgment, Tank nodded. "At the back."

"Do you mind if I leave my dog here?" I asked. "I'll be quick."

Tank shook his head. "Nope. He waits outside."

I reached down and tapped Echo on the back as he paused to snort against the linoleum. He looked up at me.

"Echo," I said. "Go wait outside." I paired the question with the hand signal for "beg."

Echo sat back on his haunches. He raised his front paws in the air, then let his wrists flop.

Good boy.

"Oh now, would you look at that," drawled Reverend Heller. "It can't hurt if he stays, can it? You're not serving food in here—what's the harm?"

"Fine," Tank snapped. "But if he knocks anything over or damages my floor, you're getting the bill."

"Great, thanks!" I signaled for Echo to stay. "Stay there —I'll be right back."

I hurried to the back of the shop. Up ahead, near the back, I could see a computer desk mounted with a flat-screened computer monitor. Tank's till system, if I had to guess. I crossed my fingers, hoping his appointment book wasn't electronic as well.

As I approached the desk, I could hear Reverend Heller lamenting the lack of dog treats in Tank's shop. I paused for a quick scan of the computer area. On the desk were the monitor, a wireless keyboard and mouse, a handheld machine to take bank and credit card payments, and a business card holder stacked with matte black cards. No book.

I glanced over at Tank. He had finished shaving the reverend's neck and was washing off the leftover foam. I nudged the mouse, and the screen lit up. No password. I looked back at Tank. He was staring straight at me.

"Need something?" he asked wryly.

"Nope!" I stepped back. "Just looking for the bathroom."

He nodded his head to the side. "To your right. Can't miss it."

I turned to look. I was less than five feet from a black door marked "Gents."

"There's no separate ladies' room," he added. "We don't get many of those in here."

"That's okay," I said with a smile. "I'll think of it as unisex."

"Whatever," Tank shrugged. He turned back to Reverend Heller.

I waited three seconds, then dropped down behind the

desk. I reached up to the mouse and navigated the cursor to the top left of the screen, where I could see a dropdown menu.

ATM... Client list... Appointments.

I clicked, and Tank's electronic appointment book opened on the screen. I squinted as I traced the cursor back over the past few days, until I reached the night of Blade's murder. When I clicked it, the day's appointments expanded to fill the screen. I scrolled down the list.

There.

One appointment on the night of Blade's murder. During the exact timeframe Blade had been killed, Tank was with Harold Bennison. The same client he and Blade had argued over.

An odd coincidence? Maybe. But it meant Tank had an alibi. And Harold could confirm it.

I clicked back a few screens so Tank wouldn't know I snooped. Now to escape unseen. Several minutes had passed, and I was too nervous to sneak a peek to see if anyone was watching. For all I knew, Tank could be glaring at the bathroom door from across the shop, counting down the seconds.

Thankfully, there was one thing I could count on. Echo would be on guard, staring at the computer desk. He would have seen me duck behind it, and I could bet my life he was watching to make sure I came out.

I stuck out my hand and made the signal for "speak." Thankfully, Tank had already put down the straight razor.

Echo's deep bark was like a bomb going off. The sound ricocheted off the walls of the barbershop and left a faint ringing in the air. Both men yelled in surprise, and I made a clean getaway.

"Sorry about that!" I called cheerfully, hurrying over to

my dog. Tank had been laying hot towels on Reverend Heller's face, and one had flung loose from his grasp and landed on Echo's head.

He shook his head, surprised, and it slapped onto the floor.

I picked it up and—with an apologetic grimace—held it out to Tank. He snatched it back, glaring at me.

"I think it's time you left," he said flatly. "And don't ever bring that dog back to my shop."

Chapter 7

A Contraband Bust

Echo

Food. The smell of it was everywhere. Wheat and egg, white sugar and milk, butter and maple syrup. The scents were warm and sweet like at the diner down the road. Pork, too, with pepper and sage. I lifted my nose as I trotted down the sidewalk next to Rabbit and took a big whiff. Put it all together, and it could only mean one thing.

Pancakes and sausages.

Licking my chops, I followed Rabbit up the short cement steps to the community hall. Whatever the job was this morning, it was going to be good.

The old wooden building was busy inside, with a few people lined up in the entryway. We'd been here several times before, always with big groups of people gathered. I did a quick scan for any signs of trouble: tension, pushing, shoving, any hotheads looking for a fight. All clear; everyone was relaxed and smiling. Most of them were hungry—I could smell it.

I glanced up at Rabbit. She'd been unusually busy the past few days, ever since we found that body. We had been coming and going from the store more than usual, and she was tracking down people and interrogating them. If I didn't know better, I'd say Rabbit was acting like a cop.

Only cops don't drink that much spicy, fruity tea.

Still, I knew one thing. She was investigating something. I'd bet my chew bone it was the murder of Big Burly Man.

Rabbit waited her turn to talk to a woman behind a small table, then she handed over a green bill in exchange for a ticket stub. I got ready to move. Whenever money changed hands in front of a door, it meant we were going in.

The hall was set up with rows of tables, and there were people sitting in chairs along the length of each one. They were all eating plates of pancakes and hot, sizzling sausages. My mouth started watering.

Rabbit took her time scouting the room. Whatever she was looking for, I hoped she would stop and take a seat. I was hungry, and I knew the drill. Humans liked you to sit nicely before they gave up the grub. I stuck by her side, ready to search and clear any chair she pointed me to.

As we walked the perimeter, I recognized a few people. First by their smell, and then by their faces. There was the older couple that ran the diner, the mailman who always gave me treats, and my favorite human in Cedar Hollow, besides Rabbit. Carpenter Man.

The other day, he'd smelled like butter, thyme, steak,

and potatoes. If I had to guess, I'd say he made a decent chef. Another reason I was happy for Rabbit to get to know him better.

I'd also been hoping he was sharp enough to join her security detail, but his test results? Pathetic. I'd run the same drill with him a dozen times. Wait for the man to be occupied, approach quietly, steal his gloves. I measured his reaction times, the steps he took to stop me, but he bombed every time. Zero situational awareness.

Still, he did have other qualities worth developing. I could sense Rabbit's heart rate slowing whenever she talked to him. He made her feel calm, happy. I could work with that.

When we neared the back of the room, I looked to Rabbit again.

What are we doing here?

She hadn't stopped to talk to anyone, and we had passed a lot of free chairs.

I gave her a quick sniff. Her blood sugar smelled low—maybe she wasn't thinking clearly. I was about to double back and signal next to an open chair when I realized where she was headed. The source of that delicious pancake and sausage smell.

Yes!

I couldn't believe my luck. She walked right up to a set of tables at the back, where people were frying pancakes on hot griddles, dousing them with syrup, adding a pair of hot sausages, and handing them off on paper plates. Leave it to Rabbit to know the people making them. Now we wouldn't even have to go sit. I wagged my tail. This shift was getting better and better.

A minute passed. No pancakes. No sausages.

Rabbit was still talking to one man, an older guy with silver hair flipping pancakes, who smelled like dusty books. He had strange clothes on. I'd never seen a human wear a little scarf stuffed under the neck of his shirt like that. The man leaned forward to look over the table at me, and then he said something to Rabbit.

Ah. I get it.

Enjoying my breakfast wasn't going to be as easy as waiting for a plate. Some humans didn't like me being around their food. I'd learned that the hard way when a lady at the diner smacked me across the nose after I decided to sample her eggs.

Rabbit often spent a long time talking to the older woman behind the counter before I was allowed through the door. And I usually had to do something to help out around the place, like when I'd saved that kid from falling over.

That's what Rabbit must've been doing now. Finding out what I needed to do to earn my meal. She was taking her sweet time, though. I looked up at her, but she ignored me.

Come on, what are my orders?

The food was right there, and I was ready to work. I decided to move things along.

I snuffled at her leg, just behind the knee. It was how I used to get Torres's attention when he had a donut or a hot dog that he hadn't shared yet.

Rabbit glanced down at me, but then she went back to talking. Message obviously not received. I moved closer to the food table and sat in front of the sizzling griddles. I looked woefully back at Rabbit. Nothing.

My stomach was starting to rumble. Time to up the ante.

I barked.

Rabbit and everyone around us reacted, including Pancake Man. His hand flew to his chest.

Finally! I knew what that hand signal meant.

Jump up.

I launched into the air and landed on one of the tables. My paws came down just a nose length away from a stack of pancakes.

Don't mind if I do.

I opened my jaws and wolfed the whole plate down.

Orders received. Job done. All in a day's work.

It was only when Rabbit hauled me off the table by my collar that I started to suspect she wasn't happy with me. When I noticed the carnage on the floor, I could see why. I'm a pretty big guy, and I guess I had knocked a few things over when I obeyed the man's command and hit the table.

There were paper plates, and broken pancakes scattered all over the floor, and an open syrup bottle had splashed onto the sausages.

A metal box was upside down at Rabbit's feet, its contents spilled everywhere. Scattered coins and bills, a poker chip, and a pack of cigarettes, which a lady stomped out from behind the table to grab.

She looked furious, barking a lot of words I couldn't hear, but I could see her mouth moving. She was waving the pack in front of Pancake Man's face.

Caught red-handed. I knew a contraband bust when I saw one.

That was a lucky find. The smell of the food was so distracting I'd completely missed the cigarettes hidden in the metal box. Good thing the man gave himself away by asking me to jump on the table. Criminals always make mistakes.

Even without Rabbit asking me to, I sat. It was time to step back and let the wheels of justice turn. This was a crime scene now, and no doubt I'd be asked to leave.

Lucky I'd managed to scoff at least half a dozen pancakes before everyone had erupted.

Chapter 8

Not A Good Look

It took a lot of convincing, but after I helped Parker Dewey, his wife, and the other volunteers clean up the mess Echo made—and parked him in a back office where he couldn't do any more damage—I was allowed to stay at the First Light Chapel's Charity Pancake Breakfast. So much for casually asking Parker to confirm whether he'd had dinner with Colleen on the night of the murder. I should have known Echo would be on the hunt for anything out of the ordinary, being a former K9. Sniffing out half a pack of cigarettes hidden in the petty cash box was as close as he was going to get to a drug bust these days.

That, or he'd been on a mission to scarf down pancakes. It was hard to tell.

Reverend Heller and volunteers from First Light

Chapel put on a charity pancake breakfast once a season on a Saturday. It was a popular event in Cedar Hollow and the surrounding towns, and it wasn't hard to see why. Pay a few bucks, enjoy some flapjacks, and go home knowing you did a good deed by supporting whichever cause The Boss had chosen. Echo and I had arrived in town just in time to miss the spring event, and I'd left him at home for the one in July. This time, I thought we'd made enough progress with our communication that I could keep him under control in a room full of people and pancakes.

My mistake.

Once the cooking station was up and running again, I spotted a familiar face coming toward me: Dahlia Monroe. Dee ran the only hair and beauty salon in town, Curl Up & Dye, which happened to be right across the street from Cal's General.

"Lucy!" she exclaimed. She wrapped a sympathetic arm around my shoulders. "The dog, the pancakes—I saw the whole thing. Don't worry, honey, it could've happened to anybody."

Dee looked glamorous as usual, this time in a gold pleated dress with hoop earrings, her dark, glossy curls spilling over one shoulder. I caught a pleasant whiff of her floral perfume as she gave me a squeeze.

"I feel terrible," I admitted. I glanced over at Parker, who was fielding the evil eye from his wife. In the few minutes I'd spoken to them, he'd seemed exceptionally meek and his wife outgoing and friendly. I hoped I hadn't caused any marital strife.

"They'll be *fine*," Dee assured me. "His wife told me they're training for a fun run, and he was supposed to quit. Honesty's the best policy, I say. Anyway, I feel like I haven't talked to you in forever. "Did you hear about Blade? Can you believe he was *murdered?*"

"Right?" I said. "I actually found the body."

Dee's arched eyebrows shot to the ceiling. "You *what?* Are you okay? No wonder your hair looks so dry. I'm telling you, you've got to keep taking care of yourself, even in a crisis. Self-care, honey. Self-care."

I smiled politely. Dee meant well, even if her delivery was a little blunt. And she had a point: I'd run out of the hair serum she sold me on my last visit to her salon, and I wasn't planning to buy more. The stuff was $40 a bottle.

"What happened?" she added eagerly. "What did you see? Was there lots of blood?"

"Sorry," I winced. "I'm under strict orders from Sheriff Annie not to talk about it."

I wasn't, but Dee wasn't great at keeping things close to the chest. Unfortunately for her clients, sitting in her stylist chair seemed to work better than truth serum.

"Huh," she said. Then her eyes widened. "Did you hear Colleen's back in town? She got here before Blade was killed. That girl's been gone for years, and now she shows up the night before her brother gets murdered."

I was almost afraid to tell her. "I've met her. We went for a walk the other day."

This time, Dee looked impressed. "Look at you! You need to come in and get your hair done more often. How are you finding out all the hot gossip before me?"

Before I could answer, Will walked over. I had spotted him when Echo and I came in, but he'd stepped out during the pancake disaster and missed the whole thing.

"I heard Echo got a little too excited about breakfast," he said. "Sorry I wasn't here to help clean up. Reverend Heller asked me to run to the store for him."

"Aw, that's nice of you, Will," said Dee, tossing him a big smile. "How are you, anyway? What's the latest?"

"I'm fine, thanks." Suddenly, Will seemed uncomfortable. He shifted on his feet, and glanced at me, then back at Dee. I'd never seen that look on his face before, but I recognized it from my own unrequited crushes over the years. The man knew he was being actively hunted.

"Now that Blade's passed away," Dee added, "*so awful*, you should come see me to get your hair cut."

Will hesitated. "You know what," he said abruptly. "I forgot my wallet." He nodded at both of us, then turned and walked out.

"Bye, Will!" Dee called after him. She giggled. "I'll keep a seat warm for ya!"

I laughed and shook my head.

"What?" she protested. "He's cute, right? You've gotta admit he's cute."

Definitely cute.

"If that dog jumps on a table like that at my diner," interrupted Betty, walking over with Boyd, "he'll be banned for life."

"I swear, he's never done that before," I protested. Echo would be devastated if he got banned from his favorite diner. "And he never will again."

"Don't be so sure," chuckled Boyd. "I saw him sitting there, looking pleased with himself."

It was true; Echo had looked ridiculously pleased with himself. The "innocent mistake" defense had been hard to argue, with him still licking pancake crumbs off his muzzle.

"We were just talking about Blade's murder," Dee cut in. "I was saying to Will, it's *so* awful."

"Terrible," Betty clucked. "You must be used to that sort

of thing though, Lucy, working for a newspaper in the big city."

"Not really," I lied. Did everybody know about my past career?

"Never seen anything like it in Cedar Hollow," Boyd agreed.

Betty *tsked*.

"Well, nothing as bad as murder, but we've had our fair share of crime," she said. "That family, the Cavanaughs, hasn't always kept things on the up-and-up, if you catch my meaning."

Boyd and Dee nodded.

I frowned. "What do you mean?"

I hadn't found a whisper of anything untoward in my research. "I thought Blade's family kept to themselves?"

Betty leaned in closer. "They did, for good reason. Blade's father, Don, used to run a bookkeeping business on the corner there, before it was a barbershop. His specialty was helping clients get creative with their numbers, if you know what I mean."

"He helped them cook the books?" I asked, eyes widening.

Boyd nodded.

"He kept things very discreet," he said. "Just shaved a little off the top for them, so I heard. For a fee, of course. He knew what he was doing."

How had I missed this? Seemed like there were a lot of secrets that I didn't know about.

"Did he ever get caught?" I asked.

Boyd scoffed. "Not Don, no. He was good at what he did. Some of his clients, though—"

"They got a little greedy," remarked Betty. "That's how we ended up with the diner."

The story sounded familiar. Myrtle had given me the short version when I'd first arrived in Cedar Hollow. "The old owner went to prison?"

Betty nodded. "That's right. We bought The Spotted Spoon for a good price, after that." She rolled her eyes toward her husband. "We could've paid less, though, if Boyd had negotiated."

"There wasn't *room* to negotiate," Boyd protested. "It was already a rock-bottom figure! They weren't going to go any lower!"

"Makes you wonder," Dee remarked, ignoring their little snit. She paused to wave at one of her clients as they crossed the hall with a plate of pancakes. "Oh, hi, Angie! Come see me for your highlights next week!"

Turning back to us, "It makes you wonder," she said again, "if Blade carried on the sins of the father."

"Oh, it goes back further than the father," Betty said, her eyebrows raised.

So there *were* criminals in the Cavanaugh family tree, like Myrtle had hinted. Clearly, I was getting rusty.

"The grandfather used to run moonshine," Boyd stated, before Betty could elaborate. "Had a speakeasy going in there during the 20s."

"Ooh, I've heard about that!" Dee said excitedly. "My great grandma used to talk about it. She said it was *really* popular. They had flapper dancers on Saturday nights, and they made the booze out in the woods past Cedar Ridge."

"Mine went once," sniffed Betty. "She told me it was a morally decrepit sinkhole full of every type of deplorable character."

"Sounds like fun!" Boyd exclaimed. Everyone laughed.

"What's so funny?" boomed Reverend Heller, approaching our group with a smile on his face. The Boss was a tall man, clean shaven thanks to Tank, and today he wore his hair slightly spiked up. The look was endearing, like a friendly rock 'n' roll dad.

"Nothing, really," Betty said sweetly. "Wonderful breakfast you've put on, Reverend. Which charity are we supporting today?"

"We're splitting the proceeds," beamed Reverend Heller, "between the fire department and the children's knitting club. The department needs a new set of tires for their main rig, and the children need yarn to knit sweaters for puppies at the animal shelter." He winked. "One costs a lot less than the other, so there's enough to go 'round!"

The group chuckled appreciatively.

"Has everyone had their pancakes already? I know Echo has," the reverend added with a chuckle. "Don't forget to enter the raffle before you go! You never know, you might win. As the Bible says in the Book of Jeremiah, 'For I know the plans I have for you,' declares the Lord, 'plans to prosper you and not to harm you, plans to give you hope and a future.'"

I wasn't particularly religious myself, but I had to hand it to him. The man knew his material. He seemed to have a quote from scripture ready for every occasion.

"And," Reverend Heller added jovially, "remember what The Boss says, too: 'Talk about a dream, try to make it real!'"

Not to mention Bruce Springsteen lyrics. I didn't know Springsteen's music well enough to pick out what song that line had come from, but I could bet the town would hear it floating through the doors of First Light Chapel before the next Sunday service.

The moment Reverend Heller walked away, Betty leaned in again. Round two. So far, this conversation had been a hundred times more informative than anything I'd dug up online.

"Did any of you see anything the night Blade was killed? Boyd and I closed up early to go to our granddaughter's ballet performance." She looked genuinely disappointed to have missed "the action."

"Lucy found the body," Dee announced. There were gasps from Betty and Boyd.

"I didn't see anyone, or anything," I said quickly.

Murmurs of disappointment all around.

"Well, I can't say I'm surprised it was a Cavanaugh who got killed," Betty remarked. "Not that he deserved it. Nobody does."

"Killed with his own razor, I heard," Boyd said grimly. "Tough way to go."

"But you're right, Betty," agreed Dee. "I never thought anybody, in a million years, would get murdered in Cedar Hollow. But with the family Blade had, it kinda makes sense. He had to have been doing something illegal in that shop."

Boyd nodded. "The apple couldn't have fallen far."

Interesting.

"His mother was a wonderful homemaker, though," Betty tutted. "My kids went to school with Blade and Colleen, and she was just the nicest woman. I have no idea how she ended up married to a Cavanaugh." She shook her head. "That side of the family was always up to no good."

Chapter 9

Busted!

Echo

It was mid-morning when Rabbit woke me from my nap. She patted her leg.

Come.

I stood and took a long stretch. Breakfast shift over. On to the next job.

After the contraband bust at the pancake table, I'd been escorted from the scene to a back office. Rabbit had asked me to lie down and stay next to a desk, and I'd been happy to oblige.

After a thorough search of the room.

There wasn't much to find. Dust. A crumpled-up tissue under a chair. An ant colony coming and going through a crack in the floorboards. Someone liked to eat ham and cheese sandwiches at the desk, and they weren't too careful about crumbs. Lucky for me.

Whoever it was liked chocolate-covered peanuts, too. I'd detected an open bag locked in the bottom drawer of a filing cabinet. Out of reach, unfortunately.

Rabbit snapped on my leash and led me out into the hall. I escorted her through the crowd at a heel. Once we were outside and clear of the front steps, she let me loose. I trotted down the sidewalk ahead of her at an easy pace, careful not to put too much distance between us.

This town was a safe town. But the murder of Big Burly Man proved what I already knew. Anything could happen.

The sun was bright and climbing higher in the sky. The air was cool, with a light breeze. Birds flew by overhead in a V, headed south. I could smell woodsmoke over a mile away, somewhere outside town. A woodstove, most likely. Traces of horse manure, too, when the wind shifted. Here, the smell of farm animals was never far away.

The walk from the community hall back to our home would take us past our store and around the corner, through the woods. Rabbit usually drove us to our day shift after morning training, but today was one of the two days in a row that we didn't work at the store. On these days, Rabbit usually liked to stay at home. She took her time doing different tasks, like talking on the phone or reading. Scrubbing the bathroom. Running the vacuum.

That monster.

I remembered the sound it made from when I was a puppy. When I'd spotted one fastened to the wall at my new home with Rabbit, I'd sprung into action. Killed it, quick and clean. Knocked it to the ground and gutted its insides.

She brought home a new one.

This time, she kept it in the closet. Wanted it there, I learned, after she asked me to leave it. Now I stayed in the bathroom when she dragged that thing out.

Rabbit made good food on days like these. Warm, rich food, meals that took time in the oven. She usually let me have a bite or two, once she was settled on the couch. My favorite was lamb chops. I even liked her carrots, when she roasted them with beef.

This morning, instead of our light run, Rabbit had asked me to escort her into town on foot. Suited me. A little variety was good for her fitness training. And it gave me the chance to get in some good sniffs.

The streets were quiet. As usual. A few people passed by, some on two wheels, most going to or from the community hall. I could still detect the salty, sweet scents of pork and maple syrup on the air as we moved down the block. Somewhere, someone else was making stew: beef with potatoes, carrots, and onions.

Up ahead was the barbershop on the corner. The crime scene. I could see light-colored police tape wrapped all the way around the building, from the front door along the side to the back alley. I would've liked to get in there and get a better look, sniff out anything the humans hadn't detected yet. But Rabbit wouldn't think of that. She wasn't a cop. The sheriff hadn't deployed me to investigate, either. Didn't know my pedigree, obviously. I could help her dig up some new leads, if she'd let me.

I caught a whiff coming from the back alley behind the shop. There was an idea. If I couldn't get *into* the crime scene, maybe I could do a perimeter sniff. Pick up a scent the killer had left behind.

Every store on the street backed onto an alley where they kept the dumpsters. Rabbit never walked me back there, but she did let me sniff around behind our store whenever she stepped out to toss the trash. Sometimes I wandered over to the next shop, and then the next. The *smells* in those bins. I wagged my tail just thinking about it.

The killer had to have got into the building somehow. If it was through the front door, my nose wouldn't help. Too many suspects. Namely, every human who had ever walked through the place. Maybe I could find something on the side, or at the back. It was worth a try.

I stopped on the street corner and looked back at Rabbit. She seemed happy that I was waiting. Not rushing to get home, from what I could tell. She held up her hand, palm facing away from me, and flicked her fingers.

Go ahead.

Green light. Perfect.

I loped across the street to start my investigation. The sidewalk itself was a no-go. Too many trace odors. Every human, dog, cat, and passing set of wheels had left molecules of their scent. I'd have to start smaller.

I approached the side of the building, narrowing my search to the concrete that ran alongside the wall.

Jackpot.

Dogs—lots of dogs—had been here. I breathed in deep. Scent profiles flooded my nostrils.

Several big males, one aggressive. The others happy. A few anxious types. Mostly healthy. Some with arthritis, one with heart disease. Elbow cancer. Poor guy. Couple of peanut butter fans.

Hold up.

Now, *this* was interesting.

Someone had eaten roast beef. A *lot* of roast beef. The whole thing, even. Probably stole it from the countertop. That wasn't all, either. Pie. Apple pie. Risky. I'd known a

K9 who lost his ball privileges for a week after swiping a glazed ham.

I snorted into the brick and moved on. Fascinating stuff, but nothing to do with Big Burly Man's murder. It was hard to know what I was looking for. A scent I recognized? Or a stranger? I rounded the end of the building into the back alley, my nose to the ground. And almost ran into someone.

I started barking.

Danger! Break-in in progress!

There was a person trying to get in the back door of the shop. She screamed when she saw me.

That's right. You're busted! Now stay put.

I advanced, still barking, and backed her against the door. Rabbit arrived beside me, puffing a little. I frowned at her. That had been a short sprint. I was going to have to dial up the intensity of her training.

Rabbit stepped in front of me and asked me to sit. I sat. She turned to speak to the woman. By now, I'd recognized who she was. Not a longtime friend, but not a stranger. Definitely not a threat.

She still shouldn't have been at the crime scene.

Now it was up to Rabbit to start digging.

Chapter 10

A Mysterious Affair

"Colleen?"

Colleen Cavanaugh was pressed against the steel back door of Blade's Barbershop, clutching her chest. She stared wide eyed at Echo, who was by now sitting calmly at my side as if he hadn't almost given the woman a heart attack.

"Is he going to bite me?" she gasped.

I bent and clipped on Echo's leash. "No, he won't. I'm so sorry he scared you like that."

Colleen nodded. "Now I know why they use shepherds as police dogs," she managed between shaky breaths. "They're effective."

That's for sure.

I had no idea how Echo had detected Colleen's presence in the back alley behind the barbershop, but I was impressed. He'd caught her red-handed, trying to break in. He looked up at me, his eyes bright, and I found myself reaching into my pocket for a treat. He wagged his tail and chomped his cookie with enthusiasm. Whatever my dog was thinking, he was clearly a step ahead of me.

"What are you doing here?" I asked. "Were you breaking in?"

"No, no, of course not," Colleen said. She unclenched her right hand and showed me what she was holding. "I have a key."

A single silver key glinted against her palm. I wasn't moved.

"Okay, but this is a crime scene. Anyone who gets inside could taint the evidence."

"I know, I know." Colleen waved her hand, looking flustered. "This is going to sound silly. But I was just trying to get Barry's affairs in order."

"Affairs?" I repeated. "His business affairs? Wouldn't a lawyer handle that?"

"Yes, there's a lawyer involved, but I know my brother. Barry's books will be a *mess*. It'll cost me hundreds in fees to have an accountant sort through it all. But I have some free time while I'm here, so I thought, 'Why not get started myself?'"

If Blade's record-keeping was as bad as she said it would be, especially given the money he owed Will, only an expert would be qualified to untangle it all. Colleen wasn't an accountant, she was a biology professor.

"So *you* were going to do the accounting," I summarized. "Before you leave town in a few days."

"Yes, exactly!" Colleen nodded, undeterred. "I thought if I could start on things, I wouldn't have such a mess to deal with when I'm back at work." She paused, then wrapped her fingers around the door handle. Echo stiffened.

"You don't think the sheriff would mind, do you, if I went in?" she asked, trying on a faint smile. "I wouldn't be long. I just want to grab Barry's files. Maybe his computer, if he used one."

"I can't let you do that," I said firmly. Not to mention Echo wouldn't have allowed her to put a toe over the threshold.

Colleen looked incredulous. "Really? I'm his sister, Lucy. I'm not going to do anything that would harm the investigation."

I offered no comment. I had no idea what she planned to do in there, but I had serious doubts that it involved accounting.

We stared at each other. Colleen frowned.

"Unless you think I want to get in there for some nefarious reason," she said, her voice clipped. "Is that what you think? That I want to get in there to *do* something to the scene of my brother's murder?" Her tone started to rise. "Like what, Lucy? Hide evidence? Why would I do that, unless you think I *killed* him?"

Colleen's face had turned red, and she clenched her fists. Echo was standing now, ready to flatten her back against the wall. I took a breath. Whether Colleen was being truthful or not, having a big blow-up at the crime scene wasn't going to help the investigation.

"I didn't say that," I answered calmly. "All I know is that it's important, really important, not to contaminate a crime scene. If you want your brother's murder to be solved, you have to stay out. No matter what."

Colleen stared at me for another few seconds. I stood calmly, my arms at my sides, one hand wrapped around

Echo's leash. His intervention was the last thing I needed. Slowly, the fury faded from her eyes.

"I see your point," she said coolly. "You're right. The most important thing is solving Barry's murder and catching whoever did this."

I nodded. "I'm glad we're on the same page."

There was a moment of silence. Colleen cleared her throat. "I guess you'll want to escort me back to my hotel to make sure I leave. I know he does." She motioned to Echo. "I can see it in his eyes."

I glanced down at my dog. His frown said it all.

"I'm sure he'd enjoy a walk," I said lightly.

Colleen nodded, and we started off. She led us back up Main Street toward the community hall, to the Cedar Hollow Inn.

The hundred-year-old building was the one and only accommodation in town, besides the new luxury villas at the Cedar Ridge Golf Estate. It had been a tavern in its original form, with a restaurant on the ground floor and two hallways of rooms upstairs for weary travelers. The interior had been renovated a few times now, but the owners had preserved a lot of the historical charm.

I had eaten at the restaurant once, when I'd first arrived. Myrtle had invited me. The steak and potatoes had been nice, but she had insisted her apple pie was a hundred times better.

Once we'd reached the wide stone steps of the inn, Colleen turned to me.

"Thank you," she said haltingly. "For being so kind. I haven't been at my best."

"You're welcome," I said. "I understand, you're going through a lot. If I don't see you before you go, I hope you have a good trip back."

Colleen nodded, then turned and went inside. Echo and I watched her go. I felt for her, I really did.

Unless she'd killed her own brother.

I'd been prepared to take Colleen's alibi at face value when we'd had our walk in the woods, but things had changed. Her excuse for trying to get into Blade's shop? I'd read better stories on a restroom wall.

Time to do some digging into Colleen Cavanaugh. Only this time, an internet search wasn't going to cut it.

Chapter 11

Neither Confirm Nor Deny

Sheriff Annie Rae Dalton didn't take Saturdays off.

On Sundays, it was common to see her walking the Cedar Hollow Trail or heading out of town to discover a covered bridge or a restaurant operating out of a historic mill. A slow Monday or a Thursday afternoon might find her hosting her twin grandsons after preschool or doing her shopping at the town's main grocery store. But every Saturday morning, Sheriff Annie's police cruiser was reliably parked outside the station while her two deputies enjoyed their leisure time.

Today was no different.

Echo and I found her in her office, door open so she could still field walk-ins to the station. She was staring at her computer, hunched over a mug of coffee and a small stack of file folders.

"Lucy," she said by way of greeting when we stopped in the doorway. "If you're looking for a story, no comment."

"I told you, I'm not a reporter anymore," I volleyed back, even though the sheriff—and everyone else in town, apparently—knew that I had been.

Sheriff Annie swiveled in her chair to eyeball me. "A little birdy told me you took a walk with Blade's sister. I didn't know you knew Colleen?"

That last statement required an answer.

"I don't," I replied. "I bumped into her on Main Street and invited her along on my walk. Turns out, she loves German Shepherds."

"That's so nice of you," Sheriff Annie remarked. "So you weren't asking her any questions about her brother's death?"

I decided not to answer that one.

She leveled me with a stern look. "I shouldn't have to tell you, Lucy, that this is a police investigation. I'm sure you were a very good investigator back in Boston, but I don't need your help solving it. I said the same thing to Myrtle Trask, and I'd hoped I wouldn't have to say it to you."

Was I that obvious?

According to the look on Sheriff Annie's face, "obvious" was an understatement.

"Of course," I said quickly. "I'm not trying to meddle."

She shot me a look that said, yeah right. "So what can I do for you today?"

I took a step forward into the office, but she put up one hand.

"Dog stays outside. He can lie down behind the front counter."

"Why?" I asked, surprised. I'd thought the sheriff liked Echo, even if she'd never come out and said it. And her sparse office, with its 30-year-old linoleum tiles, dented wooden desk, and standard blue office chairs—one behind the desk, and one in front—didn't look like it could be harmed by a few dog hairs.

Sheriff Annie lifted her mug. There was a to-go plate of pancakes and sausages on the other side.

"Because I'd like to enjoy my breakfast before he does, that's why."

I shouldn't have been surprised that the news of Echo's pancake caper had already spread, but I was a little taken aback.

"Yep," Sheriff Annie said, replacing her mug. "Word gets around fast."

I led Echo behind the front counter in the reception area and asked him to lie down and stay. He did, after performing his usual four-corner investigation. I praised him for finding the corner of a candy bar wrapper and a wad of paper that had missed the recycling bin, then joined the sheriff in her office. I settled into the chair in front of her desk.

I was going to inquire about the forensics at the crime scene, but she wasn't likely to share anything pertaining to the case after her warning. Instead, I offered up some information.

"Something happened earlier that I thought you should know about."

Her gaze flicked to me. "Oh?"

"We were just on our way home from the pancake breakfast, when Echo discovered Colleen trying to get into Blade's shop. By the back door."

The sheriff's gaze narrowed. "Did she say what she was doing there?"

"Yes, she said she wanted to get Blade's 'affairs' in order. That he was bad at bookkeeping, and she wanted to get a head start on it before she flew out."

Sheriff Annie pursed her lips thoughtfully. "Was she trying to break in?"

"Well, she had a key."

She settled back in her chair. "That sounds more misguided than anything else, Lucy. I remember when my parents passed, there was a mountain of stuff to go through. You'd want to get started on it just to get the worst out of the way."

"But why not wait until the scene was cleared?" I protested. "There's evidence in there. She could have compromised the investigation."

The sheriff nodded. "You're right, she could have. But you stopped her, so, thank you. I'm sure she meant no harm."

I found myself getting unreasonably annoyed. "Well, why try to get in while everyone in town was busy at the pancake breakfast? Doesn't that seem suspicious? It's obvious she didn't want anyone to see her."

"Lucy," Sheriff Annie said flatly. "Colleen hasn't lived here in years. Her brother was just murdered. I think there's a strong possibility she didn't even know there was a pancake breakfast going on."

"Hmm," I said, unconvinced. "Maybe."

"And this happened after you left the breakfast, you said so yourself. When was that? Fifteen minutes ago?"

"Twenty."

"So in the middle of the morning, broad daylight." Sheriff Annie tilted her chin. "Seems reasonable to me."

I bit my lip.

"I don't know. The pancake breakfast was advertised all over town. She had to know about it."

Sheriff Annie sighed. "Okay, Lucy. What do *you* think I should do about this?"

Was she being facetious? I wasn't sure.

Since she'd asked.

"I'd look into Colleen's background. Her finances. Find out if she had anything to gain by her brother's death."

Sheriff Annie snorted. "You think I'm greener than a frog's behind? I already did that."

I was surprised she'd found time.

"And?"

"And—" She trailed off. Gave a sigh, then said, "Colleen's bankrupt. She filed a few weeks ago."

I forced myself not to leap out of my chair in triumph.

"That sounds like a motive to me. She could have wanted the barbershop so she could sell it. Use the proceeds to pay off her debts."

"I agree. That does give her a motive. Only one problem. Colleen has an alibi."

My heart sank. I remembered what she'd told me during our walk. "Eating dinner with Parker Dewey at the inn?"

"How the heck did you know that?" Then she nodded. "Ah, yes. You already questioned her on your walk."

"I can neither confirm nor deny," I quipped. "But can her alibi be corroborated?"

Now it was Sheriff Annie who looked annoyed.

"Yes, Lucy, I confirmed it with Parker. And the waitress at the inn. The pair of them tipped well, if you wanted to know that, too."

I pressed my lips together. "Hmm."

So much for my lead.

"Hmm is right," returned the sheriff, arching an eyebrow. "And you claim you're not meddling in my investigation?"

I edged to the door. It was clear I'd worn out my welcome, and I didn't want to land myself on Sheriff Annie's bad side.

"I'll leave you to your breakfast," I said, hurriedly. "Thanks for humoring me, and sorry to bother you."

"Don't make it a habit," Sheriff Annie shot back. "Steer clear and let me do my job, Lucy. You're not in Boston now."

"You got it."

She was right. This wasn't Boston, and I wasn't a reporter. But this case was starting to bug me. *Really* bug me.

Both suspects had firm alibis, and the one guy I know couldn't have done it, didn't.

There was only one other person connected to the case that I hadn't spoken to yet: Harold Bennison, the owner of the Cedar Ridge Golf Estate. Blade's stolen client. It seemed like a flimsy thread, but I was out of rabbit holes to investigate.

Then, I remembered. I had a coupon.

Enjoy a $20 discount on your first golf lesson at the Cedar Ridge Golf Estate!

The offer had come in a welcome packet with my very first complementary edition of the local business association magazine. I'd also received ten dollars off a highlight treatment from Curl Up & Dye, a brochure advertising "An Afternoon Among the Autumn Leaves" hosted by a local tour bus company, and a coupon for a free coffee at The Spotted Spoon. I hoped I still had that last one, too.

As Echo and I headed down the sidewalk toward home, I pulled out my phone and checked tomorrow's weather forecast. Sunny and cool, with clear skies.

A beautiful autumn Sunday. The perfect day to take up golf.

Chapter 12

I Don't Even Like Golf

The Cedar Ridge Golf Estate was an exclusive members-only club. Sweeping, too. The grounds not only included the lush, rolling green of the 18-hole golf course and driving range, but a two-story clubhouse featuring a five-star restaurant, full-service bar, and function rooms, as well as an enclave of luxury villa accommodations nestled into the cedar trees. There was even a spa and sauna room attached to the clubhouse offering various sports massages and even "cryogenic therapy" to help the avid golfer reach "the peak physical condition required to hit your A game." Or so said the price and service menu I picked up at the gleaming front desk.

The Estates, as the place was known to locals, was a premium golfing and hobnobbing destination for politicians, visiting golf pros, and even the occasional celebrity, according to Dee. Standing in the reception area of the clubhouse with Echo by my side, I definitely looked out of place.

Thankfully, though, I was still greeted warmly by the staff. After all, I had a booking.

I had phoned the club yesterday on my walk home, crossing my fingers I could talk myself into an appointment with the owner, Harold Bennison. No such luck. He would be busy golfing that day ahead of a planned business trip that would see him leave town for a few days. The good news? He was playing on premises at The Estates. That was something.

And luckily enough for a budding golfer like me, there had been an opening for a lesson with one of the resident golf pros. A last-minute cancellation that I was welcome to fill. It was a premium playing lesson, meaning I would embark on an entire round of golf with an experienced, highly qualified instructor. Use of the club showers and sauna room afterward was included. Since I wasn't a member, the fee was an "incredibly low" $100 per hour. Reduced, thanks to my coupon, to a mere $80.

It was safe to say that I did not plan to stay long enough to play every one of the 18 holes.

"I'll show you to the women's locker room to change," the young woman at reception offered smoothly, stepping around the desk. Her name badge identified her as Holly, Guest Services.

Change? I had arrived in cream-colored yoga pants, a sage-green top, and clean white running shoes. My hair was tied up in a ponytail under a baseball cap. This was as good as it was going to get.

Holly stopped short when she saw Echo. He had been

sitting quietly beside me the whole time, and I had thought she noticed him. Apparently not. She couldn't have looked more horrified if he'd been a cockroach on a leash.

"We don't allow dogs on the green," she said, her voice suddenly sharp. "Or in the clubhouse."

"I'm so sorry," I said quickly. Silly me. I'd imagined the wide-open space of a golf course was the perfect place to give Echo his big walk of the day. Lesson learned. "I'm new to this. I had no idea. Are you sure you can't make an exception?"

I'd already paid for the first hour on arrival, and the fine print on the registration form made it clear there were no refunds. Plus, with Bennison flying overseas the next day, this was my last chance to speak to him.

Holly hesitated. I could practically see the wheels turning behind her eyes.

And the dollar signs.

"I'm sorry," she said, her voice clipped, "but he would only be allowed if you were to become a member. In which case, I could offer you the temporary dog sitting services of one of our groundskeepers."

Well played, lady.

"How much is a membership?" I asked bleakly.

An unforgivable amount of money later, I left Echo in a grassy area behind the clubhouse. His dog sitter was an enthusiastic young man wearing a branded Cedar Ridge Golf Estate ball cap and the biggest smile I'd seen in my life.

"I love dogs. I'll take great care of him!" he promised. I had a feeling Echo and I had just launched the club's latest premium service.

Now that I was a new member, Holly offered me a short tour before my lesson began.

"Yes, please," I told her. I did have some curiosity about

the spa, but I was also hoping to run into Harold Bennison somewhere in the club.

The front of the clubhouse, facing the green, was a spacious, open plan. The reception area led into a carpeted lounge with a full-service bar, where players could unwind with a drink and watch the action on the links through floor-to-ceiling windows. Between the lounge and the reception desk stood a wide staircase that led guests to the spa and locker room facilities on the second floor.

Holly walked me through the upper level, past the dry heat of the sauna and the calming reed music floating out of the spa. When we arrived back at the staircase to descend to the ground floor, Holly paused to let through a man striding out of the men's locker room.

"Good morning, Mr. Bennison," she said crisply. "I hope you have a good round today."

The man, tall with dark hair, returned her smile. "Thank you, Holly."

Harold Bennison himself. Here was my chance.

"Mr. Bennison," I said quickly, offering my hand in greeting. "I'm Lucy Hart."

Bennison didn't miss a beat. "Nice to meet you, Lucy," he said, shaking my hand. "You own the general store in town, is that right?"

"Right," I said. I was a little surprised that he knew me; he hadn't been present at last quarter's local business association meeting, the only one I had attended so far. The feeling must have shown on my face.

"I'm a loyal reader of the business association magazine. I read a profile they did about you when you took over your uncle's store. Big change of pace for a reporter from Boston."

I guess my backstory did stand out among the retirees and lifelong residents of Cedar Hollow.

"And now you've joined my club," he added with a smile. "Welcome! Or are you just visiting?"

"No, I'm a new member. I'm just about to have my first golf lesson."

"With Cole," Holly interjected firmly. "In about two minutes."

"Wonderful," said Bennison. "I'll see you out on the green, then."

He stepped past to go down the stairs. I thought quickly.

"I wanted to say I'm sorry for your loss."

Bennison paused. He turned to look at me, his eyebrows raised. "My loss?"

"Blade Cavanaugh. I'd heard you were a client of his."

"Oh." Bennison recovered his smile. "I was, yes. Such a tragedy. You never know when it's your time, do you."

"But you recently changed barbers," I pressed. "To Tank Delgado."

Beside me, I heard Holly clear her throat. Bennison seemed surprised at the statement, but he nodded. "I did."

"Can I ask why?"

"Well, I—I just preferred the way he cut my hair."

"Really."

Bennison mustered a chuckle. "I like to look sharp, and you've seen Tank. If you want the best, you go to the best."

"And you were with him the night of the murder?"

He paused. I did my best to ignore the mounting horror I could feel from Holly's direction. "Yes, we had an appointment. Haircut and a hot shave. Why do you ask?"

"Blade and Tank had a fight in my store," I said. "The day Blade was killed. It was about you."

His eyebrows shot up. "Me?"

I nodded. "Losing you as a client seemed to make Blade really upset."

Bennison took a moment to reply, as though he were weighing his response.

"Blade wasn't perfect," he said finally, "but he didn't deserve what happened to him. May he rest in peace."

Holly somehow managed to wait for Bennison to descend the stairs ahead of us before rushing me down at double speed.

"Cole's time is very important," she chided as she led me out to the practice area, a short distance from the green. "He's usually booked weeks in advance. It was very lucky that he had a cancellation this morning."

"Yes, thank you," I reiterated, speed walking to keep up. "I really appreciate it." Truthfully though, I was already wondering how to get out of the lesson, now that I'd already spoken to Bennison.

Cole, the golf professional tasked with teaching me the basics, looked around my age. He was waiting for me beside a bag of clubs, wearing a monochrome golf outfit: white golf shirt branded with the Cedar Ridge Golf Estates logo, white trousers, white golf shoes, and a branded cap, also in white. Holly had been disappointed to learn that my current clothing was the only outfit I had available, but she let me off with a warning that "proper attire" was to be worn next time. She recommended Ralph Lauren. How anyone could afford this hobby, I had no idea.

Cole and I began by discussing the fundamentals of grip. He demonstrated something he called "the Vardon" and handed me a club to try it out.

I settled my hands around the handle, then heard a familiar sound.

Barking.

My knuckles turned white. What was Echo doing?

"Good start," Cole said patiently. "But you don't have to squeeze it so hard."

"My dog," I began, then paused to listen. The barking was louder now. Excited. Nonstop. Then a yell. A frantic one.

Time to go.

"I'm really sorry." I handed the club back to Cole. "I have to end our lesson early."

By now, Cole had also picked up the sound of Echo's barking. His facial expression told me he agreed with my suspicions. Whatever was going on behind the clubhouse, it wasn't good.

"I get it," he said. "I have a Lab."

I left him to pack up and hurried out of the practice area, around to the back of the clubhouse where I'd left Echo. I turned the corner into complete chaos.

Somehow, during my absence, Echo had decided he needed to tip over and search every basket of golf balls the groundskeepers had prepared for the driving range. There were white balls strewn all over the grass. My dog was still nosing through them with enthusiasm as the young man in the ball cap scrambled around, stuffing them back into baskets. I hurried over to Echo.

"Thanks so much!" I exclaimed, touching the back of his neck. "Come on, let's go!"

Echo looked up, then his gaze fixed on something behind me. I'd seen that look in his eye before.

Squirrel.

Before I could put on his leash, Echo bolted past me and out onto the green.

"Come! Stop!" I yelled, chasing after him. He bounded

across the grass after the terrified creature, barking all the way. The squirrel had been aiming for a cedar tree at the edge of the green but somehow made a wrong turn and was stuck on the grass with nowhere to climb.

"Echo!" I screeched uselessly, convinced I was about to witness The Estates' very first woodland animal mauling. Suddenly, miraculously, Echo skidded to a stop at a sand trap and put his nose to the ground. He snuffled around, then sat.

"You," I panted as I reached him and snapped on the leash, "are a very, very, ba-"

I stopped. Sticking out of the sand was the rounded corner of something thin, like paper. I reached and pulled it out. It was a playing card, the ace of spades. I looked down at Echo. He was staring up at me, his tail swishing back and forth.

"What is this?" I murmured, turning the card over. Echo had signaled to me when he found it, I realized. He was clearly after a treat. I reached for my pockets, then remembered that my leggings didn't have any.

"Just hang on until the car," I told him, even though he couldn't understand. I could see the young woman from the front desk marching out the door toward us, looking furious. I patted my leg. "Let's get out of here."

Chapter 13

Hello, Old Friend

Monday was the perfect day of the week to deep clean the store. At least, that's what I decided the next morning. It wasn't usually, since Mondays were one of the busier days for customers. There was something about a store being closed for even a few hours that made people rush in as soon as they saw the "Open" sign.

But on this particular Monday, I needed some way to keep myself busy. Otherwise, thinking about this case was going to drive me insane.

Almost a week had passed since the murder of Blade Cavanaugh. A small-town killing with a pool of obvious suspects. And yet, no solid leads. No arrests. Even with the sheriff's warning, I couldn't stop thinking about it. I hauled out a variety of cleaning sprays and a handful of cloths. Time for a mental vacation.

Will walked in before lunch, just as I was up to my elbows in suds. As a general store, I didn't quite sell everything under the sun, but I did have one or two rows of displays for most items. Basic groceries and snacks, toiletries, office supplies and stationery. Perfect for last-minute school projects and printers that ran out of paper mid-printing, I'd been told. I also carried a selection of housewares, hardware and cleaning supplies, clothing staples—like underwear, socks, T-shirts, and hats—and even a few toys and puzzles, gift bags, and greeting cards. I'd heard from a few people that it was a lifesaver being able to grab a birthday gift on the way over to a party they'd forgotten about until the hour before.

And The Dog's Corner, of course. My favorite part of the store, and Echo's, too.

When I'd come in this morning, I'd noticed a problem in my food aisle. A few glass bottles of barbecue sauce must have been bumped somehow in transit, and I hadn't noticed when I lined them up on the shelf that their seals had popped. Now there was an overflow of sticky brown ooze that had made its way out of the bottles overnight, with some dripping down to the linoleum. On any other day, I might've groaned at the mess, but today it was a welcome distraction. After wiping it all up, on impulse I decided to scrub the whole floor. By hand. Nothing took my mind off a frustrating investigation like the voice in my head chiming, *Why aren't you using a mop?* every few seconds.

"Having fun?" Will asked when he saw me. I looked up. To my great joy, he was holding two takeout coffee cups with The Spotted Spoon logo stamped on them.

"Will Mercer. Is that what I think it is?"

"I walked by earlier and saw you'd taken on every dust bunny in here. Figured you could use a pick-me-up."

"Thank you. So much." I stood, wiped my hands on my jeans, and reached for a cup. Then I hesitated. "It's not decaf, is it? I know I said I'm not drinking real coffee, but—"

Will grinned. "I got one of each, decaf and regular, because I wasn't sure. Here." He held out a cup. "You take the regular."

"Are you sure? What about you?"

"Don't worry about me. I've got plenty of beans back at the shop."

I accepted the cup and took a grateful sip. Will had remembered how I liked my coffee from my visit the other day: cream, no sugar.

Ah. Hello, old friend.

I could feel peace settling through my body as the caffeine hit my bloodstream.

"So what's got you all wound up?" Will asked. He settled against the countertop, then reached down to scratch between Echo's ears. Echo opened his eyes, but a few more long, steady pats sent him drifting off again.

"Blade's murder," I said. "Nothing about it makes sense. For every lead, there's a dead end. For every suspect, a reasonable alibi."

Except for you.

But I didn't say that.

I still had my doubts about Colleen.

"Take me through it," Will said, taking a swig of coffee. "What's turning over in your head?"

I walked back to the front desk, then leaning against it, took a drink of my own. I liked this guy.

"First there's Tank. Blade blew up at him on the day he was murdered. Over a client, Harold Bennison."

"Yeah," Will nodded. "That was a surprise. I don't know Tank too well, but, from what I saw, Blade might've met his match. Tank wasn't backing down."

"Right," I agreed. "If you hadn't walked in—"

I trailed off. Will nodded.

"So you'd think Tank was a viable suspect," I went on. "But he had an alibi that night. He was with Bennison, cutting his hair. I confirmed it."

Will raised an eyebrow. "How did you do that?"

"You don't want to know."

Will gave a chuckle and shook his head.

"And then there's Colleen," I continued. "Blade's sister. Echo and I caught her trying to sneak into Blade's shop on Saturday. She had a key, but she was still trying to enter a crime scene."

Will frowned. "That's strange. Did she say what she was doing there?"

"Getting a head start on organizing Blade's affairs, specifically his books," I said. "Honestly, I don't buy it. Sheriff Annie told me Colleen is bankrupt. And money is a powerful motive."

"Can be," Will agreed. "Money brings out the worst in people sometimes."

"Right. But Sheriff Annie doesn't suspect Colleen at all. And she has an alibi. She was having dinner at the Cedar Hollow Inn with Parker Dewey."

Will nodded. "I know Parker. Works at the historical society. I did some work on his house a few years back." He grinned. "His wife made me cookies."

"Lucky you," I said. "I even chased down Bennison to try to get an idea of his relationship with Blade."

Will's expression told me he was fighting the urge to ask how I'd managed that. "And?"

"The man was vague at best. So that's it," I huffed. "The only other thing is that Blade owed you money. And obviously you didn't do it."

He smirked. "I appreciate that."

I didn't register the sarcasm, my mind was jumping ahead to the only other clue I'd uncovered.

"Colleen told me Blade had lined up a private buyer for the barbershop. All his financial problems were about to be solved. So why was he so mad at Tank for poaching Bennison? It doesn't add up, and it's driving me nuts."

Will contemplated this while he took a long drink of coffee. I did the same.

"You're good at this," he said finally. "Connecting the dots. I can see why you were a successful reporter."

I remembered he'd Googled me and felt the heat rising in my cheeks.

"Thanks," I mumbled.

"You should write for the local rag," he said, with a wry smile. "They could do with a decent reporter."

I was already shaking my head.

"I'm happy running the General Store."

"Your talents are wasted here," he said, glancing around at the rows of products. "One article here and there wouldn't be too much of a time suck, I'm sure."

No, it wouldn't. He was right about that.

I sighed. "I left under something of a cloud, if you must know. I don't think I'm ready to jump back in just yet."

He gave a curious nod. "Fair enough."

I liked that he didn't push. That in itself made me want to open up more.

Since moving to Cedar Hollow, I'd never really told anyone my story. As far as people knew, I used to work as a journalist in Boston, I had a dog who occasionally got himself into trouble, and I was here to run my late uncle's store. I'd alluded to having a sister and parents who were alive and well; Daphne was married with a family, and Mom and Dad still enjoyed each other's company on a good day. But that was all people knew about me.

It wasn't that I'd been purposefully secretive. Or that I was trying to keep my past hidden, like I was Echo's. I just hadn't felt like sharing yet. That was the point of a fresh start, wasn't it? Leave everything behind and start over. New home, new life. I didn't really want to get into the explosion at the drug bust, or adopting Echo, or any of the messy stuff involving the scandal I'd uncovered.

Echo came over and nuzzled my leg, before stretching out at my feet.

Will gestured to him. "How'd you end up with him? You get him as a pup?"

"No, he was older. We sort of fell into each other's lives. It's a long story."

Will fixed me with his steady gaze. "You seem to have a lot of those."

The pink in my cheeks made a reappearance. "Keep bringing me good coffee, and I might spill. Someday."

He chuckled. "Challenge accepted."

Will stuck around for another half hour. He insisted on fishing out the mop to finish the floors, despite my protests. I didn't mind. Handwashing the linoleum had been helping me settle my brain, but the coffee he'd brought had helped more.

His company hadn't hurt, either.

Once 6:30 p.m. rolled around, I was locking up when I noticed the lights still on at Dee's salon across the street.

Curl Up & Dye kept similar hours to Blade's Barbershop. They almost always closed by five on weekdays. I liked to stay open until six-thirty to accommodate locals who needed to grab something on their way home from work.

I knew the struggle too well from when I'd worked in the city. There was nothing worse than rushing to the store after work to find out it had closed an hour ago.

Tonight wasn't a repeat of last week's gruesome scene at the barbershop, thankfully. From the sidewalk outside my store, I could see Dee still working, swishing around her salon in a long black skirt with a silk blouse. I decided to go over and say hello.

"Hey! You're working late." I held open the door for Echo, since I knew Dee wouldn't mind. He wasted no time going into investigation mode, dragging his nostrils across the polished hardwood floor. Dee's salon was simple but stylish: dark-finished wood floors, tropical indoor plants with glossy leaves, and Hollywood-style mirrors lined with glowing bulbs. She'd told me that the previous owners had been heavily into the country-cute look—dried flower wreaths, barn wood panels, and cartoon cows with rosy cheeks—so she had stripped the interior down to the floorboards and rebuilt from there.

Her support had given me the nudge I'd needed when it came to renovating my own store. Namely, "Go for it and gut the whole thing." Uncle Cal had been a beloved shop owner in Cedar Hollow, but he hadn't minded doing business in the semi-dark. The old store windows had been approximately the size of a sheet of paper.

"Like *you* can talk," Dee teased. She sprayed down one of her three sinks and ran a cloth down the sides. "I saw you getting up to some hard work of your own today. With Will Mercer."

"He was just being a friend." I willed my cheeks to stay their normal shade.

"Well, I'd accept his help any day. I think he's *gorgeous*." Then, suddenly, her smile faded. "Something has been bothering me, though."

"About Will?"

She nodded. "I wasn't sure if I should say something to the sheriff, but I was thinking about Blade's murder. I may have some information."

Dee's shop was one shop over from Blade's, with The Spotted Spoon sandwiched between them. Each building was separated by a driveway, just wide enough to fit a small box truck through for deliveries. There weren't any windows in the sides of any of the shops in that block, so no direct line of sight.

"Did you hear something?" I asked. It was remotely possible. If Dee had been tossing her trash in the back alley while the murder was going on, it's possible she might have picked up the sound of raised voices.

"No. I had a client in for a blow dry that afternoon. I couldn't hear a thing." Dee hesitated. "It might be nothing."

"Or it might be something," I encouraged her. "What happened?"

"I saw Will. That afternoon. Around 4:30. I saw him come out of your store and walk by with Blade."

"They had an appointment," I confirmed. "The sheriff knows about that."

"The thing is," Dee said, "I didn't see him walk back again."

My heart skipped a beat. "What do you mean?"

Her own cheeks flushed pink. "His woodshop is down

the street, and I watch out for him, y'know? He's my afternoon eye candy. So after I saw him go by with Blade, I kept an eye on the front windows. I see a lot of Blade's customers —it takes them fifteen minutes to get their hair cut. Tops. But Will never walked back again. He didn't leave Blade's shop. Not while I was here."

Right away, I wanted to protest Will's innocence, but I forced myself to keep an open mind. I thought back to that afternoon. I hadn't seen him walk by on his way back to Mercer & Sons, either. "How can you know for sure? Maybe you missed him."

Maybe we both did.

Dee shook her head. "When I closed up at five, I looked down the street. His truck was still parked in front of his shop. He hadn't walked by, and he hadn't gone home."

I frowned. "You're sure?"

Dee's expression mirrored my own. "Positive."

Chapter 14

Main Street South

Not Will. He couldn't possibly be a suspect.

I'd been over this already. Talked to the man, heard his version of events. Crossed him off my list.

Spent time with him. Started to like him.

My brain was back in overdrive as I drove to work the next morning. Echo was belted into his harness in the back seat, his head out the window, sniffing triple-time. When I turned onto Main Street and reached the spot where I usually parked the hatchback, I kept driving. I found myself continuing up the street to the corner of Spurlock and Main. To Blade's Barbershop. The storefront, crisscrossed with yellow police tape, looked lonely and out of place among its quaint, cheerful neighbors. A ragged tear in an otherwise pretty picture.

I hit my signal and turned left onto Spurlock. Cruised slowly past the red-brick side of the shop. What I was looking for, I had no idea. Clues? Something that would explain this new information about Will? I tried to imagine him inside the shop with Blade. Having an argument about the money. Losing his cool. Committing a violent crime.

Impossible.

I heaved a sigh and flicked my turn signal again, then pulled into the next available driveway to turn around. When I reached the stop sign back at the corner of Spurlock and Main, I paused.

On the mailbox of the house across the street was painted a little gold and red book. Just like the lapel pin worn by Myrtle Trask. Myrtle, who had suffered the sound of hammers during the renovation of Blade's Barbershop.

Because she lived across the street.

Myrtle's driveway sloped upward to her white clapboard, two-story home. I turned in my seat to look at the barbershop. From her driveway, at least, Myrtle had a good view of the front of Blade's building.

But if she saw something, wouldn't she have said something already? If Myrtle had spotted the murderer from her window, no doubt everyone in town would have known by now.

But she might have spotted Will leaving the barbershop. And that would cross his name off the suspect list.

Or implicate him, depending on when she saw him leave.

I drove straight across and pulled into Myrtle's driveway. By the time I opened the car door to get out, she had appeared on her front porch, wrapped in a floral dressing gown and waving enthusiastically.

"Lucy! And Echo! Come on in, I have coffee brewing. Oh—and herbal tea."

"I'd love a coffee," I said with a smile, as Echo and I approached. "My fast is officially broken."

"Good for you, dear. We all need a harmless little vice to keep life interesting."

Even before we crossed Myrtle's threshold, Echo seemed overly eager to embark on a sniffari. Myrtle watched him fondly as he wove between the flowerpots on her porch and snorted into the shoe tray inside her front door.

"Look at him go. He must smell my cat, Nellie!" she said, delighted. "He must have been a detective in a past life."

She had no idea how right she was.

"Is Nellie inside?" I asked, glancing around nervously. The last thing Myrtle needed was for Echo to play a fun game of "chase the cat" through her lovingly decorated home.

"Oh, she's hiding on the bed upstairs. I made sure to shut her in when I saw you sitting at the stop sign, staring at my house."

I winced. "Sorry. I was just driving by, and was—"

"Thinking about the murder?" Myrtle interrupted. "Don't worry, dear, it's all I think about, too."

I followed Myrtle to the kitchen, where she poured me a cup of coffee in a mug that read, "Librarians Don't Retire, They Check Themselves Out." Her house was bright and warm, with family photos, porcelain collectibles, and shelves of books in every corner. Myrtle poured herself a cup, too. Her mug read "A Page a Day Keeps The Crazy Away". Then she topped us both up with half and half.

"So you're wondering if I saw anything the day of the

murder," Myrtle volunteered, before I'd even finished my first sip. "It's a perfectly good question, given my position." She motioned to the window over her kitchen sink, and I turned to look. Her view opened out over Main Street. I stepped closer, hoping the window looked directly down to Blade's front door. But there was a problem. From the edge of the sink, where Myrtle might actually stand to look out, a wayward cedar branch broke the line of sight.

"So the answer is no," she filled in. "Unfortunately."

I gazed out the window, letting the disappointment sink in. And then I spotted it. A white, mechanical object fastened to the trunk of the tree. It was tilted down, toward the yard. Small, discreet, but recognizable.

"You have security cameras," I gasped.

"Oh, I certainly do! There was a big, irksome tom cat that kept coming around this summer and spraying my flower boxes. I said to Nellie, 'Enough is enough!' And, well, you know." She added a wink. "It never hurts to keep an eye on things."

I'd always wondered how Myrtle seemed to know so much about the goings on in town. Now I was starting to get an idea.

"Is that the only one, or do you have others around the house?"

"Oh, I've got plenty," she said proudly. "My daughter-in-law found me a good post-Christmas deal. I've got them pointed every which way, just in case." She trailed off, realization dawning. "You don't think they might have picked up the murderer?"

She didn't wait for my answer. I hurried after Myrtle as she bustled through the house to her sunroom, barely keeping the coffee from sloshing out of my mug. Sitting open on a petite antique desk in the small, sunny space was a laptop computer.

"I record *everything*," she said, plunking down in the wooden chair behind the desk. There was no second chair, so I hovered with my coffee over her shoulder. Echo, alerted to our movement by the thumping footsteps on the floor, did a quick sniff of the room and settled into a patch of morning sun.

Myrtle clicked and navigated expertly through a series of folders to find her archive of security footage. I was surprised—the woman had definitely upskilled since the days of the card catalogue.

"Here," she announced. "Wednesday last."

She double-clicked on the relevant folder and up popped an array of video thumbnails. Each had a name like "Spurlock Corner" or "West to Community Hall." There were at least twenty files.

"Are those all camera angles?" I asked incredulously. I'd seen less coverage at a maximum-security prison.

"You can never be too careful."

She double clicked on one thumbnail labeled "Main Street South." A black-and-white video opened onto the screen. It was a perfect view of the end of Myrtle's driveway, which meant it also picked up the front door of Blade's Barbershop. I thought back to the camera on the cedar tree. The downward angle meant it couldn't have covered that area.

"Where is this camera attached?" I asked. Myrtle gave me a wink.

"The neighbor's garage, hidden under the eave. But he doesn't need to know that. What time should we start looking?"

"How about 4:00 p.m.?" I suggested. Dee had said she

saw Will and Blade walk by the window of the salon at 4:30, but eyewitness statements were notorious for being a little off. Although I'd seen Will myself just minutes before, I couldn't corroborate the time. I hadn't exactly checked my watch when Blade and Tank faced off in my store.

Myrtle dragged the cursor along the video's progress bar, speeding up the playback to quadruple time. It wasn't high-definition viewing, and the camera would have been positioned a good distance away, but I could make out the action clearly enough.

We watched the late afternoon on Main Street unfold. There wasn't much going on. Pedestrians with shopping bags, schoolkids on their way home from sports practice. A handful of cars. The reverend whizzed by on his bicycle.

"There," said Myrtle. She released the cursor to allow the video to play at normal speed. At 4:28 p.m., Will and Blade stepped into the frame and entered Blade's shop. I held my breath as the video played on. Five minutes passed. Myrtle sped up the recording.

Colleen appeared, crossing at the corner of Spurlock and Main. The day of the murder was the day she arrived in Cedar Hollow, I remembered. She would have come down the street from the Cedar Hollow Inn, which was further up by the church and the community hall.

Another five minutes passed. Colleen reemerged from the barbershop via the front door. I recalled her saying she had stopped by to say a quick hello to her brother before going to dinner with Parker Dewey. She retreated the way she came, back up Main Street toward the inn.

Ten minutes passed. Fifteen minutes. Twenty. Thirty. No Will.

"My, Will Mercer was in there a long time," Myrtle

remarked. I felt a growing sense of dread. No one else had gone in after him. "Now, when did you find the body?"

"It would have been around seven-thirty." Sure enough, at 7:27 p.m., the camera caught Echo barreling up to the door of Blade's shop. I arrived moments later, clearly out of breath and annoyed. I watched myself grab Echo and look into the barbershop window, then freeze. It was bizarre seeing the moment I had discovered Blade's body.

Even more disturbing was watching Will appear with the rest of the crowd after the police arrived. Where had he been before that?

Myrtle seemed to be wondering the same thing. "Did you see Will come out? Did we miss him?"

She rewound the footage. We watched it again. Will walked into the shop with Blade, but he never came out.

At least not by the front door.

Myrtle stopped the video. "Well, that doesn't look good, does it?"

"No," I had to admit. "It doesn't."

Chapter 15

A Cringe-worthy Moment

Back at Cal's General, I couldn't ignore the churning in my stomach.

Will had been the last person to enter Blade's Barbershop on the day of the murder. We already knew that, but when he'd left, he clearly hadn't wanted to be seen.

It was more than a little suspicious.

I couldn't prevent the tightness in my chest. With the lack of other evidence or viable leads in the case so far, it was practically damning.

But the worst part was—in all our discussions of the case, especially the ones about his movements on the night of the murder—Will had never mentioned this to me.

I'd never expected him to account for every breath or

bathroom break he took that afternoon, but the fact that he'd crept out through the back door of the shop seemed like an important detail to me.

Agitated, I bustled around my store, tidying up The Dog's Corner, trying to keep busy.

From his usual spot by the counter, Echo watched me for a few minutes through half-open eyes, before settling into his second nap of the morning.

I didn't like the idea that I could have been wrong about Will. That he wasn't the man I thought he was.

I hated that he'd withheld details from me that made him look guilty. Omitting a fact was its own type of lie. And I couldn't let that rest.

I had just decided to march over there and demand he tell me the truth, when the store bell jangled.

I glanced over my shoulder and my stomach dropped.

It was Will.

"Hey there," he called, his slow smile spreading across his face. He was holding another couple of takeout coffees.

He held one out to me. I stayed where I was.

All of a sudden, I didn't know how to handle this.

"Everything okay?" he asked, when I didn't move.

"Just had one," I croaked. "Sorry."

"No problem." He set the coffees onto the counter.

Echo, always on guard even with his eyes closed, had stood and taken a long stretch when Will walked in. Now, he chose his moment to creep around behind and launch a stealth attack on Will's gloves. But instead of playing along, Will intercepted him and ruffled his ears.

Echo didn't look too disappointed. He wagged his tail against Will's dusty jeans.

"Is everything else all right?" Will asked, when I didn't

move out of the dog's corner. A crease appeared between his eyebrows. "Did I do something wrong?"

I don't know, Will. Did you?

"I'm tired," I answered, much to my own frustration. Why couldn't I just come out and ask him for the truth? That wasn't like me.

I hoped getting to know him hadn't lost me my edge.

"And hungry," I heard myself add. "I haven't eaten well in a few days. Been up too late thinking about the murder."

There we go—the gears were spinning again. If I didn't have the stomach to talk to him here, maybe I could ease into it another way. A different setting, somewhere more public, after I had time to resurrect my nerve.

Will looked relieved.

"I can fix that," he said. "Would you like to have dinner tonight?"

My heart plummeted. Why'd he have to be so nice?

"A date?"

He shrugged. "Why not?"

Because I don't know if I can trust you.

When I didn't immediately reply, he shifted his feet. "If you don't want to—"

"No, I do," I cut in quickly. "Sorry, it's not that. It's just... it's been a while."

That wasn't a lie. I hadn't dated in years, not since my divorce. Work had kept me going, and at the time, I hadn't needed anything more than that.

He let out a relieved breath. "Okay, great."

It would give me time to work up the courage to ask him why he hadn't told me the truth about leaving Blade's the night of the murder. Or at least work out how I was going to broach the subject.

. . .

An hour after closing time, I met Will at the stone steps of the Cedar Hollow Inn. I'd decided on driving myself, which I'd explained was a basic safety precaution. If Blade hadn't been murdered, if Will hadn't held back crucial information, I wouldn't have bothered.

But things being as they were, I felt it was the safest option.

Will had agreed but looked a little deflated. I got the feeling he was a "hold the door open, pull out her chair" kind of guy. Which would have been nice, if this were a real date.

Will had scrubbed up nicely for the occasion. He was wearing a black sheepskin jacket over khaki pants and a dark-green, button-up shirt, which somehow brought out tiny flecks of gold in his eyes.

Not that I noticed.

For my outfit, I had chosen a mid-calf-length dress, forest green, cinched at the waist by a tan belt with a silver buckle. I wore black ankle boots with a low heel, and a long, caramel-colored cardigan under my black coat. Green, black, and tan. We matched. If Echo had been with us, he would have made the perfect color-coordinated accessory.

"You look great," Will said with a smile. There he was being all chivalrous again.

"Thank you."

He led me up the steps, opened the door to the inn, and waited for me to walk through. We were greeted by a bubbly brunette waitress with a name tag that read Daisy.

"Welcome to the Cedar Hollow Inn Restaurant!" she enthused, as if we were bona fide VIPs. This girl knew how to earn a big tip.

"Thanks, Daisy," Will said. "We have a reservation at seven."

A reservation. Nice touch.

Daisy showed us to our table. Despite being over a hundred years from its origins as a tavern, the inn had retained a lot of its historical charm. Stone walls under exposed wooden beams, warm, ambient light from lantern-style lamps set into the walls, and a big stone fireplace flanked by sepia-toned photographs of days past.

The tables and chairs were all solid wood, and each table featured a flickering tea light in an ornate glass holder.

Will pulled out my chair. I thanked him with a tight smile.

Say something. Start the conversation rolling.

"This is nice."

Lame.

"I thought you'd been here before." He settled into the seat across from me.

"You're right, I have. Myrtle invited me right after I moved to town."

Will chuckled. "The Cedar Hollow welcoming committee. She wanted to be the first to learn all about you so she could spread the news, no doubt."

"You're probably right. At the time, I thought she was just being friendly."

He reached for the menu in front of him. "She was, I'm sure, just with a little curiosity thrown in. Myrtle has a good heart. She was the librarian at Cedar Ridge High School when I went there."

"What was she like back then?" I tried to imagine Myrtle with a hair color other than gray.

He laughed. "She was a taskmaster. No talking in the library. Ever." He flipped to the second page of the menu. "But she got a lot of kids reading, me included."

I nodded. Suddenly, I couldn't think of what to say. "That's nice."

Lame again.

Will glanced at me, then back at the menu. I could tell he knew something was off. I had decided to ease into questioning him naturally as the evening went on, but with every passing second, I was finding it harder not to blurt out the question on the tip of my tongue.

Daisy appeared at our table and set down a basket of warm bread. "Can I get you something to drink?"

Will gestured for me to go first.

"I'll have a Coke, please," I said automatically. "Original."

"And I'll take an Amstel Light," said Will.

Daisy hurried away with our orders.

"I can recommend the steak." He glanced over his menu at me. "Unless you're not into red meat."

"I can be," I said, pretending to read the menu. Chicken pot pie, vegetarian lasagna. Did you sneak out the back door of Blade's store on the day he was murdered?

"Lucy. What's wrong?"

I gnawed on my lower lip. "Nothing."

"Come on. Are you uncomfortable here? Do you want to go someplace else?" His steady, brown-eyed gaze didn't waver. This was torture. Time to rip off the Band-Aid.

"Myrtle has security cameras," I blurted out, unable to stop myself. "She recorded something on the afternoon of Blade's murder."

Will looked surprised, but he recovered quickly. "She saw the murderer?"

"No. Well, I hope not, Will."

I left it there, giving him an opening to come clean. To offer an explanation. He didn't.

"What do you mean?" he frowned, evidently confused. "I don't follow."

"Neither do I. But I'm hoping you can clear things up for me."

He blinked at me. "How can I help?"

Here we go.

Steeling myself, I explained.

"I went over to Myrtle's today and watched her security footage. The camera picked up you going into Blade's shop for your appointment."

He gave a slow nod. "Yeah?"

"But it didn't catch you leaving. Why is that, Will?"

Will said nothing. I couldn't read his expression.

"The only explanation is that you left by the back door. Now why would you do that?"

The look he gave me was heartbreaking. "You think I had something to do with Blade's murder?"

"I don't know," I said helplessly. "I didn't think so, but then I saw the footage. Why did you sneak out of Blade's shop like you had something to hide? And why didn't you tell me about this when we talked about it before?"

He shook his head. "It's not what you think."

The uneasy feeling in my chest grew. "What isn't?"

There was a tense pause.

"Did you only agree to come to dinner with me so you could question me about how I left the barbershop?" His voice had taken on a hard edge. This was Will angry. I'd offended him, I knew that. Still, it couldn't be helped. I needed an explanation.

I didn't reply, for he'd hit the nail right on the head.

"I thought you trusted me? I thought we had something." He pushed back from the table and stood up. "But I see I was wrong."

"Will, please—"

He threw his napkin on the table.

"Since you asked, I left Blade's right after we argued, like I told you. I used the back door because I didn't want to walk past Curl Up & Dye."

"Dee's salon?"

"Yeah, Dee's salon. I didn't want her to see me. The woman obviously has a crush on me, and, frankly, she makes me uncomfortable. I've tried to make it clear that I'm not interested, but she won't quit. So I avoid her as much as I can. Last time I checked, that wasn't a crime."

I was genuinely stunned. This was Will. Of course he had a logical explanation for his subterfuge. I was the one who'd jumped to the conclusion that he'd been hiding something. I felt awful.

"Why didn't you just tell me that?"

"It's embarrassing, Lucy. And I didn't want to look like an idiot in front of the woman I like."

He stepped away from the table. "I'll pay for the drinks. Enjoy your evening."

I watched, speechless, as Will strode to the bar, paid for my Coke and his beer, then walked out.

A moment later, Daisy cheerfully delivered both drinks to the table. She blinked several times when she saw Will's empty chair. "Is he coming back?"

I shook my head, feeling my appetite go out the window.

"No."

She hovered, unsure what to do. I slowly pushed myself away from the table and got up. "I'm sorry," I said. "We won't be dining after all."

Oh, why hadn't I trusted my instincts?

Will wasn't a suspect. He was an honest, genuine, down-to-earth guy. Maybe even too much of a gentleman for his own good.

I'd messed up. Badly.

Now I'd be lucky if he ever spoke to me again.

Chapter 16

Nothing Is Ever Simple

My sneakers pounded the pavement. Five minutes into my light run, and sweat was gathering along the back of my neck and at my temples. Beside me, Echo loped along at an easy trot, barely needing to pant. If my mind hadn't been completely occupied by what had happened with Will last night, I might have wondered who was exercising who.

The early morning air was as cold and crisp as a green apple. Dawn broke as we wound through the sleeping streets of Cedar Hollow, headed for the wooded trail. From every front yard and each roadside berm, frost-covered leaves and grass twinkled in the pale morning light.

Echo made a good running companion. He stuck by my side, no leash required, keeping pace with me as we crossed at street corners and gave way to the day's first commuters on their way to work. I hadn't needed to teach him to do this, he'd come with the training installed.

Since Echo was my first dog, aside from the cocker spaniel I grew up with, I'd been grateful for that. My sister Daphne had adopted a boxer mix last year, and there wasn't leash, harness, or training technique that would stop it from pulling.

As we neared the Cedar Hollow Trail, I checked my heart rate on my smartwatch. It read 110 bpm. Not nearly high enough for how difficult each step felt this morning, or how heavily my legs seemed to drag. Running hadn't been this hard in weeks. Months, even. Today it felt like dragging my feet through mud.

I knew why. I should have trusted him, but then again, he hadn't said a word about leaving via the back door. Anyone would have jumped to the same conclusion, right?

No. A rational person would have had a civil conversation with him, not naturally assumed he was hiding something. That was the reporter in me. An occupational hazard that I clearly hadn't lost yet.

We kept going, heading for the trail that led into the woods. I'd never been a marathon runner, or even a sporty person. But, back in college, exercise had always kept me sane. It had been easy to find the time for it, too, before I'd begun my journalism career in earnest.

Even after pulling an all-nighter to study—or stay at the bar—my usual routine had been to hit the university gym or join a yoga session in the morning hours before my classes.

Like Colleen had said on our walk, everything was simpler when we were kids.

Once I landed my internship at Boston's biggest paper, everything changed. Even more so when the internship led to my first real job in the newsroom. My free time, and my routine, had vanished.

Some days, if I wanted to fit in a workout, it had to be at 3:00 a.m., after I finished churning out 2,000 words. A few extra hours of sleep, chased by a steady stream of espressos, had started to sound like a better and better choice.

Slowly, those java hits had turned from a morning ritual to an any-time-of-day necessity. At my peak tolerance, I could down a latte at 10:30 p.m. to finish a story and still pass out by midnight.

The only problem with running on fumes—caffeine fumes—was that your body wasn't as forgiving once you passed your mid-thirties. When I'd quit the paper, I'd left with a box of my personal effects, high blood pressure, and constant jitters.

Moving to Cedar Hollow had been the perfect opportunity for a lifestyle change. Along with quitting coffee, I'd made Echo—my then-new companion—a promise.

For as long as he still wanted to go running, I would take him.

Echo was nine. I didn't know how many years of good health he had left. If this old dog still had the drive to get himself out of bed every morning and paw at his leash, the least I could do was get my shoes on.

That's how I rediscovered what I'd known instinctively in my twenties. Exercise helped. It kept me fit, but it also worked out what was in my mind.

For the first time in a long while, I felt balanced. Grounded. With my dog, my store, and a few new friends, I could breathe again.

Until now.

There was no denying it. Blade's murder had thrown me.

Not the killing itself, so much. Human nature was human nature. People, for a variety of reasons, sometimes killed other people. With almost two decades of investigative journalism under my belt, it was a truth I had accepted a long time ago.

It was the fact that I couldn't solve it.

That no one had solved it. Not even the Sheriff.

Nothing about life, including death, was ever simple or easy. But this had to be one of the most confounding cases I'd ever encountered. There were no exciting lines of inquiry to follow up, or unexpected connections to piece together. There was nothing to go on. No one else to talk to.

And it was driving me nuts.

Echo and I descended into the cedar forest, the quiet still only dimly lit by the morning sun. The air here had deepened from crisp into cold. The trees seemed to be reluctant to wake up and release the chill that had fallen overnight.

My sneakers crunched on the gravel trail as we ran, turning and climbing through dips and bends. At this point in our morning run, my mind had usually cleared already, making space for new ideas. No such luck today. The cedar forest always held a certain still, solemn magic, but its powers hadn't started working on me yet.

My mind returned to last night. What a disaster.

"I admit, I could have handled it better," I told Echo, between gasping for air. I thought he'd owed me an explanation, but I totally got why he'd kept that to himself. I'd seen Dee drooling over Will, and how uncomfortable it made him, with my own eyes.

Now I owed him an apology. I just hoped I hadn't lost him as a friend.

Up ahead, I could see the other end of the forest trail, its wide mouth glowing with the brightening sun.

We'd picked up the pace. I checked my smartwatch—155 bpm. That was more like it. Each of my strides felt smooth and strong. My feet lighter. The knot in my chest was easing too. Maybe the trees had been working their magic after all. Or maybe it was just that I knew what I needed to do.

Just over an hour later, I was standing behind the counter at Cal's General, trying not to think too much. After forcing myself on my morning run with Echo and reaping the mental health benefits, the last thing I wanted to do was jump back into another spiral.

The treat bowl by the till was empty. The Dog's Corner was proving to be popular and had been patronized by quite a few canine customers since its opening. A schnauzer, a labradoodle, a giant Saint Bernard, and a very excitable Maltese mix had become regulars.

Echo had taken these four-legged visitors in his stride, rising to greet them only briefly before settling back onto his spot on the floor.

A few had wanted to play—or challenge him to a death match, in the case of the Maltese mix—but, either way, Echo wasn't interested. I could practically hear it in his sigh as he would turn around each time and go back to sleep.

I'm here to guard the store, not be their friend.

Myrtle had also been partially responsible for the bowl emptying so fast. According to her, anything and everything Echo did merited a treat. Or two.

I stepped out from around the counter and looked over my selection of Yummy Nummy dog treat flavors. Peanut butter, which I'd already offered as a sample, chicken and bacon, beef brisket, and cheddar cheese. I went with the cheese.

As I grabbed the first packet off the hanging rack and tore it open to empty into the bowl, the bell over the door jangled.

Myrtle bustled in with her shopping bag. "Morning, Lucy. I'm proud to say I've done my civic duty!"

"You voted?" I asked, distractedly.

The treat bowl refilled, I reached down to get Echo's attention. As a rule, he liked cheese, but I knew his favorite would be chicken and bacon. I was trying to hold out as long as possible before introducing him to that flavor. Once he clued in that bags of delicious treats were hanging on a peg a few feet away at all times, the pawing and pleading looks were going to be nonstop.

"No. I went to see the sheriff."

I stopped. "The sheriff? Why?"

"You know? The evidence." Her voice had dropped to a conspiratorial whisper. "The surveillance footage."

Echo, now awake and aware that I'd wanted his attention, sat up and stared at me, waiting for his next command. I stared back at him, my heart plummeting.

Oh, no.

"Sheriff Annie was just delighted," she went on enthusiastically. "She's been under a lot of pressure to make an arrest."

I felt my blood go cold. If she looked at that video, she'd have every right to haul Will in for questioning again, and this time it might not go so well.

Echo frowned up at me, his black brows rumpled.

It was imperative I solve this case, before Will got arrested for something he didn't do.

Chapter 17

The Phantom Podcast

There were some core tenets in investigative journalism that every good writer subscribed to, policies that separated tabloid magazines and sensationalism from trusted, reputable reporting. The first was to protect the anonymity of your sources. The second was to back up alibis and witness statements as much as possible. And the third was to fact check everything.

With no new evidence or leads, I focused on two and three.

Colleen Cavanaugh's alibi was the only one I hadn't personally verified. The sheriff had accepted her story about the night of Blade's murder at face value. According to Colleen's version of events, she had been having dinner that night with her friend Parker at the Cedar Hollow Inn.

I'd wanted to speak to Parker about the dinner at the First Light Chapel's Charity Pancake Breakfast over the weekend, but Echo's appetite had derailed that line of inquiry.

I had a feeling that, after the pancake fiasco, gaining Parker's trust was going to take a lot of work. Especially since Echo had busted him smoking cigarettes behind his wife's back. Instead, I decided to go back to where their dinner had supposedly taken place: the restaurant at the Cedar Hollow Inn.

I chose my moment just before 2:00 p.m., after the usual crowd of locals on their lunch breaks had come through my store for snacks or afternoon treats. I slapped the "Be Back in Five" sign on my door and patted my leg for Echo to come.

"Come on, old man. Time for a walk."

I'd learned early on that leaving him behind in the store was a bad idea. His view down the street through the glass door meant he could watch me walk away, then bark continuously until I relented and came back.

Just before locking up, I doubled back into the store and used a black marker to multiply the number of minutes I'd be away. My new sign read: "Be Back in 30." Might as well be honest.

After snapping on Echo's leash—no time for squirrel chasing or sniff breaks today—we hurried down the sidewalk to the Cedar Hollow Inn. Echo was clearly wondering what the deal was; at the pace I was speed walking, we were practically jogging. When we arrived at the inn, his tail started wagging. He could probably smell the remains of the lunch service wafting through the door. Poor guy looked positively horrified when I tied his leash around the leg of a bench outside and asked him to stay put.

"Sorry," I said, producing a treat from my pocket. I

didn't have time to waste getting kicked out of another establishment serving food. At least, not before I got my answers.

When I walked into the inn, the restaurant was quiet. Only a few lunch guests lingered. An older couple sharing a chicken pot pie and a trio of colleagues drawing out the end of their lunch hour at the bar.

"Welcome to the Cedar Hollow Inn Restaurant." Daisy was working again, but seeing me, she wasn't quite as bubbly as she'd been the night before. There were no menus this time. She also politely avoided acknowledging the events of last night. "Our kitchen is actually closed now until dinner, but you're welcome to enjoy a drink at the bar."

"Daisy, I was actually hoping I could speak to you," I said, trying to be friendly.

She looked around nervously. "My manager doesn't like me standing around for too long. What is it about?"

"Were you working last Wednesday night? The night Blade was murdered?"

Daisy's eyes widened. She glanced over her shoulder at a middle-aged woman standing in a crisp button-up shirt behind the bar.

"Gimme a sec. I'll go on break."

I waited for Daisy out front where Echo was waiting, so we'd be out of earshot of the bar and the elderly couple. She joined me less than a minute later, her cheeks flushed. "Are you investigating the case."

"Not officially," I said, wondering at her enthusiasm.

"Oh." She looked down at Echo. "I thought maybe you were an undercover police officer, or a detective working the case."

I hesitated.

"Well, I suppose you could say I'm investigating the case in a different capacity."

"Ooh, like for a podcast?" She didn't wait for me to answer. "I *love* true crime. I mean, it's awful what happened to Blade, and I'd never wish death on anybody. But how crazy is it that a murder happened right here in Cedar Hollow!"

Ah. A true crime fanatic.

"So you were working last Wednesday night?" I prompted, trying to refocus her.

She nodded eagerly. "I work almost every night. There's one other girl who works here, and we're supposed to split the shifts down the middle, but I'm trying to save up for a new car, so she gives me most of them. I don't think she minds too much, she's got rich parents."

"Colleen Cavanaugh," I interjected gently. "Do you remember her having dinner here that night?"

Daisy thought for a second. "Yeah, she's staying upstairs. She was here with Parker Dewey, just the two of them, until around seven. Maybe just before." Her eyes widened. "Is he cheating on his wife with Colleen?"

"Not that I know of," I said quickly. Parker would never speak to me again if I sent that rumor swirling around town.

Another flash of disappointment.

"They were both here all evening?" I asked again, just to make certain.

"Do you mean including if they went to the bathroom? Or—"

I smiled. "I mean here in the building. Bathroom breaks not included."

Daisy took another moment to think, but this time she shook her head. "Colleen stepped out for a phone call. A long one. I remember because when she got up and rushed out the door, I was worried she was dining and dashing."

"Does that happen a lot?" I asked, surprised.

"No. I'm pretty sure it's actually never happened." She tilted her head toward the bar. "My manager is paranoid about it, though. So I had to make sure. Colleen said it was her daughter on the phone from Europe. Something about the time difference meaning she had to take the call *now*, while she was still awake."

"Do you remember how long she was gone for?"

"Maybe ten minutes. She and Parker were having appetizers when she left, and I delivered the main course when she got back."

So Colleen had left the table—and the premises—for ten minutes. I thought about that for a moment.

Was it enough time to get to Blade's shop, kill him, and make it back to finish dinner?

Daisy leaned forward.

"What are you thinking?" she asked conspiratorially. "Do you think Colleen did it? That she killed her own brother?"

"No, of course not," I said quickly.

She stuck out her lips. "What do you think happened, then? It must have been a frenzied attack. I heard Blade was stabbed twelve times."

Jeez. The Cedar Hollow rumor mill seemed to have gone into overdrive.

"His throat was cut," I corrected her. "Probably with his own razor."

Daisy's eyes widened. "Wow. So it wasn't premeditated?"

I frowned. "Why'd you say that?" May as well talk shop with someone as interested in the case as I was.

"Well, they didn't take their own weapon. They used one that was already there. That means it was a crime of opportunity."

I contemplated this. She had a point.

"Or the killer could have known there would be a razor there they could use. I mean, it is a barbershop."

"Colleen would definitely know," Daisy said, her gaze narrowing. "She was his sister."

"If she had enough time," I said, forgetting I was supposed to be squashing rumors, not starting them. "She only had ten minutes to dash along the sidewalk to the shop, go inside without anyone seeing her, kill Blade, then get back to the table before you brought out their main course."

"Don't forget change her clothes," Daisy pointed out. "Blood spatter. Especially if she got close enough to use the blade."

This girl was good.

"Unless she slit his throat from behind," I said, thinking out loud. "The blood would have spurted forward, not back and onto her clothes."

"Still pretty risky," mused Daisy. "Arterial blood would go sideways, but I guess it's possible."

We sat in silence for a moment, contemplating the scenario. Daisy was right. The timeline was tight, but doable.

Over Daisy's shoulder, I could see the woman in the button-up shirt eyeing us from behind the bar. It looked like the clock on her break was about to run out.

Daisy saw her too and stiffened. "I'd better get back to work."

"Thanks for your help," I said, and meant it.

Daisy grinned. "You're welcome. Can't wait to hear the podcast."

. . .

I called the sheriff's office on my speed walk back to the store, Echo in tow. He was unimpressed that I'd returned without any leftovers.

"I have new information," I said, when Annie picked up. "It's about Colleen."

"Lucy, what a nice surprise." Her tone stated that it clearly wasn't.

"I spoke to the waitress at the Cedar Hollow Inn restaurant," I said, forging ahead. "Her name's Daisy. She was working the night of Blade's murder, and she confirmed that Colleen had dinner there with Parker Dewey."

"I know all this," came the taut reply. "Listen, I have to go. I've got a suspect in custody."

My heart wrenched. "Not Will," I whispered hoarsely.

"I saw the footage," she continued. "As I'm sure you did. Will is now a person of interest in this case."

"Will didn't do it," I insisted. "If you'll just listen to what I have to say."

"I heard you. They were there all evening."

"Not all evening."

There was a brief pause.

"What do you mean?" she asked, eventually.

I took a shaky breath. "Daisy remembers Colleen stepping out for a phone call that lasted at least ten minutes."

"Daisy used a stopwatch?" asked the sheriff.

"No. She noticed because of the timing of the appetizers and the main course."

Echo skidded to a halt at the street corner, narrowly stopping me from stepping in front of an oncoming car. I took a quick breath and dug a treat out of my pocket.

Good boy.

"Okay," Sheriff Annie said slowly, "so she stepped outside for ten minutes. I've just received security footage of the front entrance of Blade's Barbershop from the night of the murder, and Colleen isn't on it."

"Myrtle's camera set-up isn't perfect. You can't see into the back alley behind the barbershop. It's possible that Colleen snuck around there somehow when she left the inn and went in and out through the back."

"The same way Will came out?"

"Yes, exactly. Ten minutes is enough time to commit the murder and rejoin Parker at the Inn. It's tight, but it's possible. Plus, she has a motive—her bankruptcy filing. Now that Blade's dead, she can sell the store and reset her finances."

There was a pause as the sheriff considered this. I could tell she knew I was right.

"I'll have another word with Colleen," she said, finally.

"You'd better hurry. She's due to leave tomorrow."

"Then I will speak with her tonight." She sounded weary, and I felt sorry for Sheriff Annie. This was probably the biggest case she'd had in her life. A real homicide, right here in Cedar Hollow.

In Boston, they had teams of cops looking into a murder like this. Here, it was Annie and two deputies. Maybe that's why I felt so compelled to help.

I thought about Will in police custody and my insides twisted. Hopefully this information would show Annie that he was innocent. That there was another suspect. Someone who had just as good a motive to want Blade dead.

The afternoon hours dragged by at an excruciatingly slow pace. I was desperate to know what had gone down. Had the Sheriff taken Colleen into custody? Had Will been released?

Hopefully his name would be cleared, and justice could finally be served.

As the clock ticked closer to 5:00 p.m., I glanced out of the window and saw two sheriff's vehicles drive past the window, lights flashing.

Uh-oh. That was never a good sign.

I glanced at the clock for the fiftieth time that afternoon. It couldn't hurt to close early, just this once.

When I arrived with Echo outside the inn, the chief medical examiner's van was parked outside, as was the sheriff's cruiser and one of her deputies' black-and-whites. I spotted Daisy sitting with a deputy on the bench to which I'd tied Echo earlier that day. She was wrapped in a shiny foil shock blanket and giving a statement.

I felt a pulse of dread. What had happened?

I jogged up the steps of the Inn with Echo, ignoring the deputy's startled command to keep back. If he came after me, I'd leave, but I had to know what had happened. I heard voices and police radio chatter coming from the top of a staircase.

Echo and I rushed up.

At the top of the stairs was a landing that branched off into two hallways. Down the hallway to my left was a crime scene.

Two officers stood outside an open guest room, its doorway blocked by yellow police tape. One of them was Sheriff Annie.

"What happened?" I asked, hurrying over. She stared at me with a mixture of disbelief and dismay.

"Lucy! What are you doing here?"

Echo was looking intently through the doorway, his nose twitching. I followed his gaze, just in time to see the lifeless body of Colleen Cavanaugh being zipped into a body bag.

Chapter 18

A Change In Direction

"Colleen's dead?"

I couldn't hide my shock. I'd expected Sheriff Annie to be questioning her, possibly making an arrest, not facing another murder.

Two men wearing jackets that read "Office of Chief Medical Examiner" were handling the body. They busied themselves strapping the body bag to a gurney to be wheeled out.

"Yes," Sheriff Annie said curtly. "Now get—"

"How? And when? When did this happen?"

"We think within the last hour, based on body temperature," the deputy answered. Sheriff Annie shot him a look.

"Did anyone see anything? Hear anything?" I glanced around the room, trying to take in as many details as I could.

There had clearly been a struggle. The bed looked disheveled, and there was an upturned suitcase on the mattress. Clothes were strewn on the floor. An occasional chair by the window had been turned on its side.

Colleen must have been packing to leave when she was killed.

"Lucy," Sheriff Annie said firmly. "I need you to—"

"Her phone," I interrupted, pointing. A smartphone was lying on the floor by the bed, half under the base of an overturned water glass. The screen glowed through a speckling of wet droplets. "Look, it's unlocked!"

Sheriff Annie's gaze pivoted to the phone. She knew as well as I did a victim's mobile phone was a treasure trove of information. And normally it would take days, even weeks, of police time to crack the passcode. In one smooth movement, Sheriff Annie lifted the police tape and ducked into the room. She reached for the phone, then stopped.

"Does anyone have gloves? Or an evidence bag?"

"The forensic guys are on their way with both," answered the deputy. Sheriff Annie glanced at me. We both knew this couldn't wait. I reached into my pocket.

"Here, it's clean."

She hesitated for a split second, then accepted my offer of a new, unused dog poop bag. Opening the thin plastic around her hand, she carefully picked up the phone. Drops of water slid off the screen. The water had kept the phone unlocked, but hopefully it hadn't done any lasting damage.

Sheriff Annie carefully examined the phone. From the doorway, I could see that it was open to the keypad, as if Colleen had been trying to make a call.

"Looks like she was halfway through dialing my number," the sheriff said quietly. One of the chief medical examiner's men produced a clear pair of latex gloves from the depths of his bag, then gingerly took the phone. He swiped to Colleen's settings to disable her passcode.

"Check her calls and texts," I suggested. "See if she invited anyone to come and see her."

Sheriff Annie looked ready to fire back a retort, then thought better of it and directed the CME's man to access Colleen's text messages. If Colleen had been expecting someone to drop by her room at the inn, the sheriff could be tracking them down and making an arrest within the hour.

"No plans by text," she reported, mostly to herself. "A text from Blade the day of the murder, asking when she was arriving in town. Parker Dewey making dinner plans the same night. Then checking in a few times after the murder. A couple of local numbers. Old high school friends, looks like. Offering condolences."

That was nice. It seemed Colleen had died with a few more friends in town than she'd arrived with. "What about the call log?"

She directed the man to check Colleen's list of recent calls.

"Find anything?" I prompted.

Sheriff Annie thanked the man from the medical examiner's office, then unfolded the bag around the phone so that it dropped inside. She swiftly knotted the top. "No. Her last few calls were to an international number. Before you ask, yes, she received a call from the same number last Wednesday night, when Blade was murdered. From France. It lasted ten minutes and thirty-three seconds. Happy?"

Happy wasn't the right word. Finally, once and for all, the call confirmed Colleen's innocence in the murder of her brother. She'd been on the phone with her daughter in Europe when he'd been killed, just like she had told Daisy.

But confirming her alibi didn't just mean Colleen was innocent. It meant we were completely out of leads on Blade's murder. And now his sister was dead, too.

I finally made myself scarce, leading a disappointed Echo away from the scene and out the door of the inn. As I jogged down the front steps, I saw that Daisy was still there. She was alone now on the bench, still wrapped in the foil blanket and clutching a mug.

"I found the body," she said haltingly, when we walked over. Steam rose from her mug and dissipated into the fading afternoon light. I sat on the bench next to her. Petting Echo's soft, furry head seemed to have a therapeutic effect on me, so I hoped it would do the same for her.

"That must have been awful," I sympathized, remembering the shock I'd felt when I'd seen my first dead body, shortly after I'd started at the newspaper. Nothing prepared you for that.

One of Daisy's hands drifted idly down the back of Echo's neck. He wriggled closer for more.

"The sheriff came to talk to Colleen," she recounted, her voice shaking. "I took her up there myself, since it was quiet in the restaurant. We got to Colleen's door, and—" She shook her head, unable to continue.

"It was open?" I prompted gently. "Ajar?"

"Ajar," Daisy nodded. "Sheriff Annie called her name, but there was no answer. She asked me to step back, then she pushed open the door. That's when we saw her."

"On the floor? The bed?"

Daisy swallowed. "Half on the bed. Hanging over it, kind of. I knew right away something was wrong. She wasn't moving. It was weird. I never realized how much people move when they're alive." Daisy blinked back tears.

"Her eyes were bloodshot, and there were red marks on her neck."

Sounded like she'd been strangled. Whoever had killed Colleen, they had wanted it done quietly. Just like whoever had murdered Blade.

"I've watched a lot of shows about this stuff," she said. "It's so different seeing it in person. I knew Colleen. I served her at the restaurant. It's terrible."

I gently rested one hand on Daisy's back, my palm crinkling the foil blanket. "Can I call someone for you? Someone to come and pick you up, if the police are done speaking with you?"

Daisy shook her head. "Thank you. The deputy already called my boyfriend. When he gets here, they said I'm free to go."

There was a metallic rattling noise, and I looked up to see Sheriff Annie stepping through the door of the inn ahead of a covered gurney. Colleen's body. The black body bag I'd seen in the room was now covered by a white sheet. The two men from the chief medical examiner's office escorted the gurney through, one at each end. Together, they lifted it slightly and eased it down the steps, wheels clattering against the stone.

"I'm guessing the manner of death was strangulation?" I said as they passed. I hoped the sheriff would at least correct me if I was wrong.

"How did you guess that, exactly?" She glanced from me to Daisy, who busied herself petting Echo.

"Just a hunch," I said vaguely.

I watched the men load the body into the back of the van. The double doors closed, and they jogged around to the driver and passenger side doors. The sheriff went back inside the inn, leaving a deputy to stand guard at the door. I got the feeling from Sheriff Annie's parting look that his purpose was to keep me out, specifically.

"Is your boyfriend almost here?" I asked Daisy. She nodded.

"He just texted me. That's him now." She rose and shrugged off the foil blanket as an old red Honda Civic pulled up a little ways down the block. I followed her gaze. And then it hit me.

Colleen had stepped outside the inn to use the phone the night Blade was killed. From out here, she would have had a view down Main Street to Blade's Barbershop on the corner. It couldn't have been more than a quarter mile away. And she wouldn't have seen just the front. The side of the building, too, alongside Spurlock Road.

I sat up straight. What if she'd seen someone that night when she took the call. Someone going around to the back of Blade's shop?

What if she'd seen the killer?

Chapter 19

The Real Deal

"Mind if I join you?"

I'd stopped by The Spotted Spoon on my way to work the following morning, and who should I see sitting quietly in a booth, a folder open on the table in front of her, but Sheriff Annie.

She seemed to be deep in thought, her coffee growing cold as she shuffled papers in the folder, so I thought twice about interrupting.

Just not too hard.

I needed to tell her my theory, because it was a good one.

Echo had followed me inside and stood beside me, his tail thumping on the table leg. The sheriff looked up, frowned, then said, "Sure, why not."

I slipped in opposite her and tried to peer at the documents in the folder. It looked like a forensic report from the crime scene. I tried to read the writing upside down and got as far as "no forced entry," before she flipped the folder closed.

"I take it there's a reason for this impromptu visit?"

"Actually, I was just stopping in for coffee, but then I saw you. There's something I wanted to run by you."

She lifted an eyebrow. "Oh yeah? What?"

I nodded to the folder. "Got any leads yet?"

She stared at me, not answering.

"Okay, fine. I think I know why Colleen was murdered."

Annie blinked, then frowned. "You think you know? How could you possibly know? You'd only just met her."

"Yes, but yesterday, when I was outside the Inn talking to Daisy, I realized I was standing in the exact spot that Colleen would have been standing in when she took that call from her daughter. The one in Europe."

Annie's gaze narrowed. "So?"

"Well, from out front, you can see directly down the street to Blade's Barbershop. Not only that, but you can also see down the side road that leads to the alleyway that goes to the back entrance."

I let that sink in.

Annie's voice dropped to a whisper. "Are you suggesting Colleen saw Blade's killer?"

I gave a firm nod. "That's exactly what I'm saying. It's possible, right? The timing fits. She may well have spotted whoever snuck around the back to murder Blade."

I leaned forward. "What if the killer noticed her? What if they were worried she'd be able to identify them? So they silenced her."

I straightened up, breathing rapidly. My pulse was faster than it should be, and I hadn't even had a coffee yet. Echo must have noticed because he nudged my leg as if to say, "are you alright?"

I patted his head, just to prove that I was fine, then looked back at the Sheriff. She was thinking, her fingertips drumming on the table.

"It's a possibility," she allowed, and I breathed a sigh of relief. "But I'm going to need more than that."

"What about cameras at the Inn?" I asked. "Maybe they picked up Colleen's killer going inside."

"Now why didn't I think of that?" she said, sarcastically.

I grimaced. "Sorry, old habits."

"We're going through the footage," she said, relenting. "But it could be any one of the numerous diners and guests that entered through the front that day."

"No camera at the back?" I asked.

She shook her head. "I shouldn't be telling you this."

I leaned back and crossed my arms. "I'm only trying to help. I know you're short staffed and overworked, and I'm good at this investigating thing. I used to do it for a living, remember?"

"How can I forget?" she countered, with a quick grin.

Then her expression grew serious. "Listen, Lucy. While I appreciate the effort, it's not safe for you to be looking into these murders. There's a double-killer out there, or if it's not one person, then there are two perpetrators on the loose, and I don't want you putting yourself in danger."

She had a point, but I wasn't an amateur. I'd been down this road before, several times. Back in Boston, on some of the bigger stories for the paper, I'd tracked down a host of unsavory characters. I knew the risks, and I knew how to manage them.

"I appreciate your concern," I said, "But I know how to look after myself. Besides, I've got Echo. He's the best guard dog anyone can ask for."

Echo gave a soft grunt of agreement.

"See?"

She gave a thin smile. "Why are you doing this? It can't just be to help me out?"

I thought about that for a second. "I guess it's just part of who I am," I said, eventually. "I tried not to get involved, but when it happened on my doorstep, well it was just too hard not to."

She shook her head. "I can't share information with you about an active investigation, you know that right?"

"I know, but there's nothing stopping me from sharing what I find out with you, is there?"

She shook her head, the corners of her mouth tugging upward. "No, there isn't."

The day's trade at the store was slow. That was normal for a Thursday, but it didn't make it any easier to get through. I paced around the shop floor, keeping busy by tidying and rearranging shelves I'd already cleaned and organized earlier in the week.

Echo watched me from his sunny patch on the floor, his eyes half open, his black brows furrowed. I wondered if he felt just as frustrated as I did. Not only was I fixating on the two murders, but the situation with Will was still playing on my mind.

I hadn't seen him yet to apologise, and now with Colleen's death, I'd been somewhat preoccupied. But that was something I had to do soon. I didn't like that he was mad at me.

I was pleased when Myrtle decided to stop by for a visit. She was always a distraction. As soon as she walked in, she went right for the bowl of dog treats.

"Here boy!" she called to Echo, snapping her fingers.

I stepped closer and gently nudged him with my foot. He opened his eyes, spotted the treat in Myrtle's hand, and went right into a picture-perfect sit.

"How are you, dear?" Myrtle asked me, once Echo had gobbled three treats in short order. My chicken-bacon reckoning was approaching fast. "I can't believe there's been a *second* murder. I just hope all this death hasn't put you off living here."

"Not at all," I said truthfully. Figuring this thing out was making me feel like my old self again. Minus the jitters.

"Do you know what happened with Will?" I asked her. "Last I heard, he was being questioned by the Sheriff on account of that footage you showed her."

"Oh that." She waved a hand in the air. "Sheriff Annie released him almost immediately. I'm not sure what explanation he gave her, but he's no longer a suspect."

Her level of intel never ceased to amaze me.

Another thought crossed my mind. "Myrtle, did you know Colleen when she used to live in Cedar Hollow?"

"Only from her time at the high school," Myrtle said. "She was a good student, from what I can recall. Better than her brother at returning her books on time." She *tsk*ed and shook her head sadly. "No one deserves to go that way. By the hand of another."

I nodded in agreement. I was about to ask her something else when through the glass panel in the door, I saw Will stride past. My heart gave an involuntary little jump, and I knew I had to act. I couldn't let another day go by without talking to him.

"Myrtle, can you keep an eye on the store. There's something I've got to do."

She followed my gaze, then gave a knowing nod. "Of course, dear. You go right ahead."

I dashed out into the street. "Will," I called.

He stopped, turned and looked at me.

I hurried over to him. "Listen, Will. I'm sorry about the other night. About what I said. I should have trusted you. It's just, I can't seem to help myself." I shook my head helplessly. 'I know that's not an excuse, but I really am sorry."

He exhaled slowly. "Thanks, Lucy. I'm sorry if I got defensive. I guess I was embarrassed."

I smiled at him. "Friends?"

He gave a nod. "Friends."

"Great." I hovered for a moment. "Hey, I've got to get back inside, but do you want to meet for a coffee later?" I'd missed my morning brew on account of talking to Sheriff Annie.

"I've got a better idea," he said. "I've got a quick errand to run, then I'll pick up two from The Spotted Spoon and head over to yours."

I grinned. "Sounds perfect but make it three. Myrtle's there."

"Gotcha." He gave me a wave, and I hurried back to the store, already feeling the tightness in my chest lighten.

Myrtle and I were still talking about Colleen, and the company she used to keep when she lived in town, when Will reappeared with three takeout coffees as promised. I fell on mine with a delighted squeal.

He chuckled. "I see you're off your tea kick?"

I took a sip and closed my eyes, savoring the taste on my lips. "I'm back to the real deal, but only one a day. Maybe two. But no more than that."

Myrtle removed the lid and blew into her cup. "Speaking of coffee, didn't I see you this morning at The Spotted Spoon with Sheriff Annie?"

Will's eyes turned to me.

"I wasn't drinking it, I wanted to talk to her," I said, a tad defensively.

He grinned. "No one's judging you." Then his smile faded, "I heard about Colleen. Do you think her death is related to Blade's?"

"Almost certainly," I said with a nod.

"What are the chances of two murders in one small town being unrelated?" Myrtle added, raising an eyebrow.

She was right. They had to be.

"Do they know who did it?" Will asked, frowning.

I shook my head. "No, but I can tell you there was no forced entry to her hotel room. She must have let her killer in."

"Which meant she knew them," Myrtle finished with a flourish.

"Exactly."

"Annie tell you that?" Will asked, his gaze on me.

I shrugged. "I may have read it on the forensic report she had open on the table."

He shook his head as Myrtle cackled. "I knew I liked you the moment you arrived in town," she said.

"There was something else," I added. They both looked at me expectedly.

"I talked to the waitress, Daisy, and she told me Colleen left dinner on the night of Blade's murder to take a phone call. She was outside for ten minutes between appetizers and the main course. I went and stood outside, where she'd have taken her phone call, and I could see right down the street to the barbershop."

Myrtle gasped, putting it together immediately. "You think she saw Blade's murderer?"

"I considered it," I said. "But there's one problem with that theory. Why wait over a week to silence her? If the killer knew Colleen had seen them, then why not take her out right away?"

"Maybe she didn't realize she'd seen the killer until later?" Will offered.

"But if *the killer* knew they'd been seen, even if she didn't know what she'd been looking at—" Myrtle shook her head gravely.

I thought back to what Annie had seen on Colleen's phone. She had been halfway through calling the sheriff's department. If the killer had been standing there in the room with her, they might have acted out of desperation.

"And if Colleen had known them, it makes sense that she would have let them into her room."

I glanced at the clock on the wall. Come closing time, I wanted to go back to the Inn and have another look around. Hopefully the room wasn't still closed off, or if it was, there might not be anyone there and I could slip in unnoticed.

Not that I thought they'd missed anything, it would just give me a clearer picture of what went down.

"I'd better get back to the workshop," Will said, draining what was left in his cup.

The door jingled as a mother walked in with two small children. Myrtle put her cup down on the counter.

"I'll walk with you," she said, casting a look in my direction. "See you later, Lucy. We'll reconvene tomorrow and see if there's anything new."

I had to smile. Myrtle was treating solving the murder like another one of her book groups. Between her and Daisy, Echo and I were in good company.

Chapter 20

Scent Of A Murder

Echo

R abbit needed my help.

Yesterday, she'd dragged me to the inn. Twice. With no job to do. No treats to earn. The first time, I'd saved her from getting flattened by a car, and the second, I'd had to let some girl cry on my fur.

Still, she gave me a few good head scratches, so it wasn't all bad.

That was the day the cops found another body. I thought it was a violent death, since the place was wrapped with police tape. I'd taken a whiff as the victim went by. Middle-aged female. No diseases. No fresh wounds or blood, either.

Two dead humans now. That was two more than I'd expected to run into in this town.

I had another gripe about that day. My dinner had been late.

Rabbit nearly forgot to feed me when we got home from the inn. She was never sloppy when it came to my meals. I always got a big bowl of kibble with a full can of meaty gravy, as soon as we walked through the door. I counted on it.

I knew the signs. The same thing used to happen to Torres when he was in the middle of a case. Rabbit was preoccupied with the investigation, and it was messing with her head.

I'd lain in my usual spot on the floor of the store all afternoon, watching as Rabbit, Carpenter Man, and Treat Lady conducted a briefing.

Rabbit wasn't a cop, but she was an investigator, and she obviously relied on their intel. Suited me. I wasn't much of a thinks-things-over kind of guy. I liked getting out there, putting my nose to the ground, working the crime scene. I enjoyed hunting down perps.

With Rabbit's approach, there was a lot of talking.

As a fellow law enforcement officer, I had to respect her methods. Torres had had his own way of doing things, too. Still, I got the feeling Rabbit was chasing her tail.

There'd been no arrests yet, as far as I could tell. No big excitement or celebrations for a case closed.

It was time I got more involved.

I stood guard by the door, waiting as Rabbit did her final rounds and set the security code. When we stepped outside, she put on my leash and asked me to escort her down the street. It didn't take me long to figure out where we were headed.

Back to the inn. The scene of the second murder.

Yesterday, neither of us had been invited to inspect the crime scene. Maybe we were finally being called in.

Wagging my tail, I trotted down the sidewalk next to Rabbit. Enough talk. Time for some action.

As we approached, I could smell food. Hot food. Chicken and potatoes. Steak and gravy. Even lamb chops. A line of drool slipped out from the corner of my mouth.

Any other night, I'd have been in there like a flash, finding out exactly what I had to do to get some grub. But now, food could wait. Rabbit and I were on duty.

I started up the steps of the inn, then felt a tug on my leash. I turned to look at Rabbit. I couldn't believe what I saw.

She was pointing to the bench. The same one she'd tied me to yesterday. She wanted me to stay out here. Again.

I stayed put, staring at her. She couldn't be serious. How was I supposed to help her further the investigation from out here?

Rabbit tugged on the leash again and pointed to the bench. She patted her leg, asking me to come.

No way, lady. Not sitting this one out. Not this time.

Rabbit was holding tight onto my leash. She wasn't backing down, either. I considered my options.

I could make a run for it, still attached to Rabbit. That wouldn't end well, for me or for her. On my end, the leash would slow me down and make it easier for someone to catch me. On hers, she would faceplant onto the stone steps and probably break her nose. Since my job was to protect her, that obviously wasn't an option.

The alternative involved a bit of trickery. No problem. I'd deceived people plenty of times before. Treat Lady fell for my "I'm starving" face every time. Getting one over on a human was easy, if you knew how to do it.

And I had a plan.

Dutifully, I backed down the steps and maneuvered to Rabbit's side. I made sure to look sad but resigned. Accepting my fate. That was key. I wanted her to think I was going to obey her command, but I also wanted her to feel bad about making me wait. Nothing like the sad puppy dog face to get sympathy.

Rabbit reached down and ruffled my ears, as if to say, *good boy*. She gave me a few long strokes down my back and a couple of thumps on my ribcage for good measure. This was her way of apologising.

Now take me to the bench.

Rabbit walked me over and bent down to tie up my leash. With her center of gravity off balance, I strained at my collar, making the leash taut. She wavered, struggling to get the end of the leash tied around the bench.

She touched me on my neck, and we stared at each other.

Sit, she commanded.

I did, but as far away from the bench as I could. She tried to tie up the leash again, but no luck. I'd made sure of that.

After thinking for a moment, she grabbed my collar with one hand. With the other, she unfastened the leash. She was going to loop it around the bench first, by itself, then clip me back on. I knew because she'd done it before. Only this time, I wasn't planning to stick around.

I yelped, as if she'd stood on my foot. Rabbit jumped away, distressed, and let go of my collar.

Oh no! I'm so sorry, Echo. I imagined her saying. *You poor dog. Let me see your paw.*

I took off and bolted up the steps to the inn. Following my nose away from the smell of food, I dashed up a set of carpeted stairs. A few people reached for me as I ran past, but I dodged them. This was my chance to investigate the crime scene, and nothing was going to slow me down.

I skidded into the first hallway off the landing and zeroed in on the crime scene. It was easy to spot. Light-colored tape still crisscrossed the door.

There was a deputy outside, standing guard. He looked shocked to see me, but I couldn't blame him. He'd probably never worked with a K9 officer of my caliber before. I made sure to give him a friendly nudge as I zigzagged around his knees and into the room.

There was a forensic officer processing the scene. They were dusting for prints. My nose hit the carpet. Time to join the team.

The scene was a standard bedroom. Big bed, nightstand with a lamp, chest of drawers against the wall with a TV on it. A chair—the big, stuffed kind—lay on its side in the corner signalling some kind of altercation.

The sheets were pulled off the bed, and there were clothes all over the floor. I lifted my paws onto the mattress and saw an open suitcase with the contents spilling out.

I sniffed around the edge of the room first, then the bedding and clothes. A water glass, then the overturned chair. That deputy was hot on my heels. He kept running after me as I moved, sticking to me like a shadow.

Never mind. I was happy to teach these small-town cops a thing or two.

Most of the room smelled like the victim. I remembered her now. Rabbit and I had walked with her in the woods. There was another scent here, too. Another person. The strongest hit was on the overturned chair.

The night of the murder played out for me as I weaved between the deputy's legs and worked through the smells.

The victim had been here in the room. Touching the clothes and the suitcase. The killer had come in, sat in the chair. Then they'd got up again, attacked the victim. There was a struggle.

I breathed in deep.

Every killer leaves a piece of themselves at the scene, and this one was under the bed. I crouched down on my haunches and wriggled under the bed. With one swipe of my tongue, the evidence was safely in my mouth.

Just in time, too. Someone grabbed hold of my tail and yanked. Turned out it was that deputy. Talk about conduct unbecoming an officer. He was lucky I was holding evidence, or I'd have introduced him to my teeth.

Rabbit was there now, making a lot of muffled sounds. I trotted over, waiting for a pat and a treat, except she snapped on my leash and pulled me away from the crime scene.

I expected her to slow down once we reached the sidewalk so I could give her my evidence, but she powered on.

Maybe she hadn't noticed me collect it.

I dug my claws into the concrete and forced us both to a stop. Rabbit turned to me, her mouth still moving. I noticed she was red in the face, and her blood pressure was high.

This wasn't good.

She signaled for me to come, but I didn't. Instead, I gazed at her, my mouth closed.

It took a second or two for her to realize I had something. She crouched down in front of me and held out her hand.

Finally.

I dropped the evidence into her palm. She looked at it for a moment, then reached into her pocket for a treat.

Good boy.

Chapter 21

The Mysterious Buyer

A button. My dog had brought me a shiny black button.

Standing behind the counter at Cal's General the next morning, I laid the button down next to the other odd item Echo had sniffed out this week.

A playing card. The Ace of Spades, to be precise. It was weathered and creased at one corner, as if it had been well used but had no other marks on it. I had no idea why a playing card had been sticking out of the sand at the Cedar Ridge Golf Estate, let alone why Echo had wanted me to see it.

The button from Colleen's room looked completely ordinary. It was medium-sized, four standard thread holes, with a slight ridge around the edge. It could have come from a cardigan, a suit jacket, or even a dress.

Had it belonged to the killer?

Was it Colleen's? Maybe it had come off in the struggle. I tried to envisage what she had been wearing on the occasions I'd met her, but I didn't remember the button detail.

Was it even a clue, or just a wayward bit of trash that the inn's vacuum cleaner had missed from the last guest?

A button and a playing card. Either Echo was following his K9 training and turning up evidence, or he was part packrat.

I shook my head as I looked down at him. Sweet as an angel, pretending to be asleep in his usual spot on the floor. I rolled my eyes as a tiny snore escaped his snout. The doggy devil in disguise.

Yesterday's mad dash into the crime scene at the Cedar Hollow Inn had been a disaster. I'd barely gotten through my front door when I'd fielded a call from an irate Sheriff Annie threatening to boot me out of town.

She had every right to be angry. Echo had run all over her crime scene, likely contaminated evidence in the process. "That dog is out of control," she'd told me. "Why wasn't he on a lead?"

"He was, but he manged to get away," I'd protested, after apologising profusely. It wasn't the first time this week that he'd run amok.

Only me promising never to walk him around town without a lead eventually pacified her.

I sighed. I didn't know what had been going through Echo's mind last night when he'd broken free and run into the inn, but one thing was sure. He'd been on a mission. I knew it was far-fetched, but it was almost like he'd gotten loose for the express purpose of reaching that crime scene.

I glanced up at the clock. It had been a busy morning at the store, but it had quietened down now. As promised, Myrtle stopped by to talk about the case. I had to smile as she bustled in, tote bag over one shoulder.

I told her what had transpired the evening before, and she chuckled. "I can just imagine the furore he must have caused." She patted Echo's head and gave him a treat.

I showed her the button. "This was what he found under the bed."

Myrtle hunched over the counter and studied it. "I can't say I recognise it from anywhere," she said.

I hadn't expected her to. Who notices the color or style of people buttons? I sure didn't.

With no new leads to follow up on, she left, saying she had to get to book club which was held once a week at the public library.

Back at the paper, when investigating had been part of my job, I'd done it for two reasons. One, I loved the work. Two, it brought home the bacon.

Here in Cedar Hollow, I obviously wasn't getting paid for all these extracurriculars, but I couldn't ignore the fact that it felt right. Like a calling.

I liked the idea that I might be able to make a difference here.

Sniffing around these murders seemed to make Echo happy, too, and whether he was finding real evidence or just hoarding trinkets, I didn't know, but I wasn't going to stop now.

"Wakey-wakey," I told Echo, reaching down to get his attention. I grabbed his leash and patted my leg, and he was on his feet.

"If we're going to figure this thing out," I told him, "we need coffee."

As we stepped out of Cal's General, I noticed a stranger standing outside Blade's Barbershop. The crime scene tape had come down a few days ago, after the police had finished processing the scene.

He was a short guy in his mid-to-late forties with brown hair under a wide-brimmed hat. He wore a calfskin jacket, black tee, dark jeans, and round, gold-rimmed glasses. I pegged him as an artsy type, but with money. Like a kid who'd grown up loving comic books and now owned all the first editions.

He seemed to be lurking on the street corner, outside the barbershop, so I decided to go and find out who he was.

"Good morning!" I said brightly. "You look a little lost. I'm Lucy Hart, I own the general store across the street."

His face lit up.

"Digby Ridgely," he said, breaking into a goofy grin. "Man, I love this town. You guys are all so friendly."

"Can I help you?"

Digby bobbed his head toward the barbershop. "I was in talks to buy this place and turn it into a coffee shop with my daughter, but things have gone a little quiet, so I decided to come down here and see what had happened."

I quickly connected the dots. This was Blade's private buyer. The one Colleen had told me about who was prepared to shell out more than the place was worth. Looking at Digby, and the fond way he was gazing at the barbershop, it made sense.

"Oh, I'm sorry to be the one to tell you," I said. "But Blade Cavanaugh was mur— er, died, which is probably why you haven't heard anything."

He paled as my words registered, then I saw a crushing disappointment settle over his expression. "I—I had no idea. I'm so sorry to hear that."

He stared at the store as if trying to figure out what had occurred there. "How did he die?"

The question I'd been avoiding. "Um, he was murdered. The sheriff is investigating. If you want more information, you should probably go and talk to her." I'm sure Annie would want to have a word with Blade's prospective buyer too.

"Oh, yeah. Of course, I will." He nodded several times. "Excuse me, this has come as something of a shock. We were looking forward to closing on the deal."

"I'm sorry," I said, only because he was so dejected by the news. If Colleen was still alive, Digby could have purchased it from her, but she was dead too. I had no idea what fate awaited the barbershop now, but I suspected it would involve months of probate and expensive lawyers.

Still, I wanted to find out more about Blade's buyer before he headed off to talk to the sheriff. "How did you and Blade meet?" I asked. "Have you been to Cedar Hollow before?"

"One time, during the summer. That's all it took," Digby said, a wistful gleam in his eyes. "I make movies—I'm a producer—and we were on location a few towns over. One day, I took a drive with the crew, and we ended up here. Got myself a haircut, met Blade, and fell in love with the place. He said he'd be interested in selling, so we struck a deal."

"Are you thinking of retiring here?" I asked, intrigued as to why a movie producer would want to run a coffee shop in a small town like Cedar Hollow.

"Kinda," he said. "My daughter's been wanting to open a cafe, and I was saying how much I loved the decor he had in there. That 1920s style, man. I love it. Art deco, all that luxury and clean lines. There was so much art back then."

I nodded. Definitely an artsy type. If he did buy the

barbershop, it would be competition for The Spotted Spoon. I wonder how Betty and Boyd would feel about that.

"Blade was listening to me rave about how much I loved his shop, and he said he wouldn't mind selling it, for the right price," Digby went on. "So I went for it." His smile faltered as he surveyed the shadowed front window. "Don't know what's going to happen now, though. Crazy that the guy got murdered. Who would have thought *that* would happen."

So Blade had offered to sell the barbershop almost on impulse. It sounded like the act of a man desperate for money.

Buy why? Even though he'd owed Will a few thousand dollars, his debt didn't seem impossible to afford. Especially not over a whole year. Had business really been that bad?

"I'm sure whoever's handling Blade's estate will be happy to speak with you about it," I said. "Sheriff Annie will be able to help you with that."

He broke into another lopsided grin. "Let's hope we can salvage our dream. Thanks, Lucy. It was great meeting you."

"Good luck," I said, smiling. "I hope we meet again."

He nodded enthusiastically. "I'll be sure to come into the general store and say hi, next time I'm in town."

We parted ways, and I went back to work. Echo was waiting for me inside, peering through the glass panel with distain. I felt like he was judging me for leaving him behind.

"Hey, old man," I said, as I walked in. "Thanks for watching the store."

He grunted and went back to his bed in the dog corner.

. . .

Echo glanced up seconds before the door jingled. He had this ability, even deaf, to sense when a customer was about to walk into the store. Except this wasn't just any customer. Will stood there with two coffees in his hand and a rolled-up piece of paper underneath his arm. His eyes were sparkling as he walked over to the counter, and I felt irrationally pleased to see him.

"Hi," I said, grinning at the smile on his face. "You're spoiling me."

He set the coffees down. "I've come to show you something." He held up the long roll of yellowed paper.

"Building plans," he said, unfurling it on the counter. "Old ones."

The edges of the paper were lightly tattered, and there was a brown coffee ring near one corner. The fine lines and letters, in purplish-blue ink, were still easy to read. Will held the paper flat with one hand and ran his palm along the plans with the other.

"This is the original floor plan to Blade's Barbershop," he said.

"The original?" I arched my eyebrows. "Are there others?"

Will gave a knowing nod. "Oh, yeah. City Hall has the floor plan of every business in Cedar Hollow, and they're available for anyone to look at. So I did."

"What made you want to do that?" I asked.

Will shrugged. "I've been listening to you and Myrtle run through the evidence, and it's clear we're missing something. I thought maybe the answer was in Blade's shop. And since it's locked up, I thought I'd start by looking at the plans."

I was impressed. Sometimes it paid to have a man around.

Glancing down at the plan, I asked, "What did you find?"

"The ones at City Hall? Nothing. They seemed too new. There were features that were only added to the building code in the last few decades—and everybody knows the Cavanaughs have owned that place since the 1920s."

Doubly impressed. "You tracked down the originals?"

Will nodded. "Found them in some old, dusty storage room under City Hall. The strange thing is, they're different."

I narrowed my gaze, interest duly peaked. "Different how?"

Will pointed to a small rectangle of floor space on the old plan. It had been shaded with diagonal lines.

"That room, there. It's under the main floor, accessible by a set of stairs."

My eyes widened. "A basement?"

"More like a cellar," Will decided. "That in itself isn't unusual, but what is, is that someone would have had to have pulled a few strings to get it left off the updated plans."

We gazed at each other.

"Blade's shop has a secret underground room," I said, slowly. "I wonder what he used it for."

Chapter 22

The Secret Door

Just after lunch, a van with the words *Crime Scene Cleaners* on the side trundled by Cal's General.

I poked my head out the door to catch some of the action, but I couldn't see much. Just a standard white van and a couple of guys in dark blue overalls going in and out of the barbershop.

I wasn't the only one watching. A small crowd had gathered outside the store. I smiled as I saw Myrtle at the front.

I wondered if this was Digby's doing? Maybe whoever oversaw the estate had agreed to get it sold off as soon as possible, since Blade's debts weren't going to go away. It seemed pretty quick for lawyers, though. These things usually took much longer. Then again, money talked, and Digby had seemed pretty keen on the café idea.

By the time I closed up my store, the cleanup crew had finished their work and vacated the premises. The view down the street looked exactly like it had a few weeks ago, before the first murder.

Dee's salon across the street, her neon pink sign switched off for the evening. The Spotted Spoon, its 'closed' sign flipped against the window. And Blade's Barbershop, quiet and empty, its windows dark. Still, nobody would forget what had happened there. Not for a long time.

Will met me outside, as I was locking up. Our plan was to take a peek at the basement room, if we could get inside the barbershop. It had been my idea, and to my surprise, Will had gone along with it—even though we could get into trouble if caught.

I leashed Echo, and we made our way with Will across the street. We ducked down the driveway beside Curl Up & Dye and popped out into the back alley that ran behind the entire block of shops. The early evening light was fading, perfect for our purposes. The autumn sun had officially set only ten minutes before, and with each advancing minute, the sky deepened into darker and darker shades of blue.

We walked quickly down the alley, past each solid wall of red brick. None of the backs of the buildings had any windows, just a door and a pair of bins each. One was for garbage, and the other recycling. Echo was intent on thoroughly investigating each one, but I encouraged him along with a light tug on his leash. When he looked up at me, his brow rumpled, I gave him a treat for keeping up. I was counting on Echo's protective instincts—and his nose—to keep watch for us while we checked out the basement of Blade's shop. The least I could do was pay him for his time.

The back of the barbershop was unchanged since the

last time I'd seen it, the day Echo and I had prevented Colleen from breaking in.

Will pulled his gloves out of his back pocket and put them on. "Stand back, please, Lucy," he instructed, trying the door handle.

"What are you going to do?" I had no doubt the man had strong shoulders, but the door looked pretty robust.

To my surprise, he pulled a screwdriver out of his other pocket. "I just need some elbow room."

He began by prying off the faceplate of the door handle, exposing the screws that held the mechanism together. One by one, he unscrewed them and slipped each into his pocket for safekeeping. Within minutes, he'd dismantled the handle enough to slide the latch aside and unlock the door by hand.

"Wow," I remarked. "You're handy to have around."

"Try to be." He grinned as he pushed open the door using the heel of his hand, then stepped inside first. "All clear."

Echo and I followed him in.

The interior of Blade's shop was almost exactly as he'd left it. Black leather barber's chairs, dark wood paneling on the walls, and gilded art deco fixtures and finishings. Absent were the hair products, disposable neck strips, protective capes, and bottles of spray.

I guessed the cleaning crew had tossed all of that stuff.

There was a strange stillness to the place, more than the usual quiet of a business after hours. No hum of electricity behind the walls or ticks from the radiators. I had expected the air to smell strongly of bleach or ammonia, but there was no odor. The cleaners had done a thorough job.

There was only one noticeable difference. Or rather absence. The chair Blade had been killed in was gone.

Instead, an empty circle remained on the floor, branded by large screw holes.

"We need to find the hidden entrance, Will said, stepping over to one of the wooden wall panels and giving it a light tap with his knuckle. It sounded solid.

I knocked on the panel closest to me. Solid again.

Echo moved along the wall, nose to the ground. He stopped as Will tried another. That one sounded hollow. He pushed it, and one edge bumped up, lifting the wood away from the wall.

We'd just found the secret door.

Will edged his fingertips underneath the wood. Slowly, with a long creak, he pulled the door all the way open.

We were met with a cold draft and the dark mouth of a stairwell.

Will was about to go down the stairs ahead of me, but I put out an arm and stopped him. "Let Echo check it out first, just in case."

He quirked a brow. "The place was locked up tight. I'm pretty sure no one's hiding down there."

Echo knew his role and glanced up eagerly at me. He was a trained police dog who knew how to handle himself. Plus, it was the perfect opportunity to give him the employment he craved.

"Please," I said, lowering my tone. "It'll make his day."

Will stood aside. "Okay, in that case..."

I unclipped Echo from his leash. He barreled down the stairs, his tail whisking against both walls and disappeared into the darkness.

Will turned on the flashlight on his phone, and we listened for any sounds of trouble. No barking, no growling. Nothing. Just soft snuffling as Echo felt his way around the space.

"I think we're good to go," I said.

The passage was narrow and dark, like a servant stair-case I had once explored during a tour of a historic home. I walked down easily, but Will's broad shoulders came close to grazing the walls. I imagined Blade stepping down these stairs at an angle, since he was easily several inches wider than Will.

The wall plaster was smooth in sections, but patchy and crumbling in others. Each step groaned under our weight, but they held. Will led the way at a slower pace than I would have liked, especially given the cobwebs dangling into the beam of his flashlight, but I had to give him credit for being safety conscious.

He was no doubt making sure neither of us tripped and took the rest of the stairs face first.

As we reached the bottom, I could hear Echo's claws clattering against the floor as he made his rounds. Will's flashlight lit up the open space, and he let out a low whistle.

"Would you look at this?"

We were standing in what looked like an old wine cellar. The floor was covered in faded linoleum with a geometric pattern, and yellowed green and gold paper peeled from the walls. I immediately thought of Digby Ridgely and his enthusiasm for the 1920s. He'd love it down here.

The length of the room was lined with shelves. Most were empty, but some held a few gallon-sized ceramic casks sealed with a cork.

There was a long, rectangular patch of missing linoleum on one side. Thinking back to what Betty, Boyd, and Dee had said about Blade's grandfather, and what he'd got up to during the roaring twenties, I guessed that the patch was where the bar had once stood.

"I think we found the old speakeasy," I whispered.

The space wasn't huge, but it was large enough to host a few dozen patrons. Well hidden from the police, and deep enough underground to muffle any sound. Blade's grandfather would have been free to serve his moonshine to a small, secret clientele.

In the middle of the room, under an old-fashioned hanging lampshade, was a round wooden table. Eight black folding chairs were pulled in around it.

In the middle of the table stood an open black box stacked with colorful discs.

"Poker chips," Will murmured, stepping over for a closer look.

I circled the table, studying the chips.

"So, Blade was running an underground poker game. Literally."

"Organized poker is illegal in the state of Vermont," Will remarked. "All professional gambling is, unless you're a charity or a nonprofit. Even then you need a special license."

"Really. I didn't know that." Massachusetts law was completely different. "Do you know the penalty?"

"Not off the top of my head. A few years of jail time, maybe. A big fine."

Blade's volatile temper, probably due to his high-stakes financial pressures, were starting to make sense.

"This could be where Blade's money troubles started," I theorised. "Maybe he organized the poker nights just for fun, but he ended up with a few big losses he couldn't pay. Add that to the renovations he'd already done on the place, and his bills were starting to pile up. Not to mention these games were illegal. That always comes with the risk of getting caught."

Will nodded. "Explains why he was so tightly wound before he was killed. Why he went off at Tank over losing one client."

"He was digging himself into a hole," I muttered.

The grim implication settled over us. That hole had turned out to be his grave.

Chapter 23

*We Weren't Breaking
And Entering*

Will and I didn't spend long in the cellar. Although no one in Cedar Hollow had any real reason to walk through the back alley after hours, there was always the chance that a random passer-by would happen along and notice the back door was missing its handle.

After taking one last quick poke around, I leashed Echo, and we made our way back up the stairs.

Will closed the wood panel behind us, and we exited the way we came in. Echo stood guard as Will put the door handle back together. Thankfully, nobody had decided to take an evening stroll down the alley. We were in the clear.

"The poker den has to be tied to Blade's murder," I mused as we headed back down the alley. The daylight had faded, and the indigo twilight was descending over the town. The streetlights had come on, allowing us to see the way back.

"Money problems can make people do desperate things," Will agreed. "If someone had a gambling debt they couldn't pay—"

I stared at him. "That's a powerful motive for murder."

I thought back to what I knew about Blade's clientele. Before Tank had arrived and opened Straight Edge Cuts, odds were that most of the town had gotten their hair cut at Blade's Barbershop. That meant any number of people could've been quietly invited to the game, depending on who Blade handpicked to join.

Then it hit me. Who better to take part in a poker game than a wealthy man?

"Bennison," I stated as we emerged into the street beside Dee's store.

"Huh?" Will glanced over.

I clicked my fingers. "That's the reason why Blade was so angry. Not because he'd lost a client, but because he'd lost one of his poker players. The richest one."

"Maybe Bennison threatened to talk?" Will said, frowning.

I turned the idea over in my mind. "It's possible, but why would Bennison switch barbers in the first place? If he was part of the gambling ring, why would he leave Blade and get his hair cut at Tank's instead?"

"He could have wanted out," Will suggested.

I reached into my back pocket and pulled out the playing card Echo had found at the Cedar Ridge Golf Estate. The Ace of Spades. It had come from Bennison's golf course, but dozens of people walked the green every day.

Still, I was betting it belonged to him.

"What's that?" Will asked.

I handed him the card. "Echo found this at the Cedar Ridge Golf Estate—in a bunker. At the time, I thought he was just after a treat for finding something weird in the sand, but now I'm wondering if it belonged to Bennison. Maybe it had something to do with the poker games."

"Could be," said Will, his forehead furrowing. "But didn't you tell me Bennison had an alibi?"

I gave a tight nod. "He had an appointment with Tank during the timeframe of the murder. But, if he was involved in the poker game, he would have a lot of valuable information to share with the police."

He nodded. "What are you going to do?"

"I could talk to Bennison again," I said. "See what he has to say?"

Will frowned. "If he's involved, that could be dangerous. You could speak to Sheriff Annie... tell her what we've found."

I started to shake my head. "She's going to be so mad we broke into the barbershop."

"Don't mention that part," he said. "Tell her about the plans. I acquired those legitimately. They clearly show the hidden cellar."

I perked up. "Okay, that works."

He grinned and gave a little nod. "I'd come with you, but I've got to work. Keep me posted?"

I smiled. I'd enjoyed our little adventure. "Will do. And thanks, Will. This has been really helpful."

He tilted his head in acknowledgement. "No problem."

Sheriff Annie's gaze slanted the moment I walked into her office. I could see the alarm bells going off in her head.

I held up my hands. "I'm not here to cause trouble, but I do have some information to share with you."

She looked behind me, expecting to see Echo walk in beside me, but I'd tied him up outside. I wanted to stay in Annie's good books, and unfortunately, Echo had priors. That meant leaving him outside.

She gestured for me to sit.

I sank into the chair opposite her desk and said, "Blade Cavanaugh had a hidden cellar in his barbershop. I think he was hosting illegal poker games down there."

I waited for my words to sink in, knowing it would get a reaction.

Annie stared at me for a long beat. "And how did you come across this information?" she eventually asked.

I gulped, hoping she couldn't tell I was skirting the truth—kind of. "Will found the old floor plans to the store, and we saw the cellar on those. There was talk of a speakeasy, back in the day, so we thought maybe it was from that."

So far, so true.

She gave a slow nod. "I had heard that rumor."

"Oh, it's not a rumor. Myrtle and both Betty and Boyde confirmed it."

That narrowed glance again. "I see."

"I think you should take a look," I prompted.

"What makes you think Blade was conducting illegal gambling?"

The question I was dreading.

"Just a guess," I said. "Echo found this playing card at the golf estate the other day, and it would explain why Blade was so upset that Tank stole his customer. It wasn't just because he wanted the business, it was because he was a big spender at the poker table."

"That is a massive assumption," Annie said, studying me. "What aren't you telling me?"

"I may have asked around," I said, deliberately vague. Hopefully, she'd think someone had gossiped about the gambling den.

She sighed and fished in her desk drawer for a set of keys. "Okay, I'll go and check it out."

"Great, I'll come with you." At her stern look, I added, "What? I'm heading that way anyway."

She rolled her eyes.

Echo was grateful for another trip to the barbershop. This time, we didn't have to take off the door handle. Annie let us in with the key. I waited as she glanced around, trying to pretend like I hadn't just been here the night before.

Echo had no such qualms, though. He headed straight for the panel that led downstairs to the cellar and sat staring at it.

"Looks like he might have found something," I said, realizing this was all a little too convenient. Annie must have thought the same, because she frowned as she came over.

"How'd he know this was here?"

"Instinct," I said, firmly.

I knocked on the panel. "Sounds hollow."

She felt around, then as Will had done the night before, released the mechanism and pulled the hidden door open.

I gasped in mock surprise. "I knew it."

She shot a suspicious glance in my direction, but before she could say anything, Echo had darted down the steps.

Even with the daylight filtering in from up the stairs, the light was too dim to see clearly. I looked around for a switch. There was one embedded in the wall, so I flicked it and the cellar was flooded with bright light.

"You were right," she breathed, walking around and taking everything in. "There was gambling going on here."

I nodded, standing back so she could inspect the chips.

"I'll have to get the crime scene officers back in," she said. "Although, there are probably a host of different prints in here."

"It will tell you who was involved," I remarked.

She gave a somber nod and took out her phone. "No reception." She gestured to the stairs, and we ascended back to the main floor.

Leaving her to make her call, I went back to Cal's General, just in time to open for the woman with the golden retriever. She'd been patiently waiting for me to come back. This sleuthing was getting in the way of my day job.

When Myrtle came in for her daily dose of gossip, I filled her in on what had happened. As expected, the news greatly delighted her. "I knew it," she whispered, excitedly. "I knew he was up to no good. It's in their blood, you know."

I was beginning to, although Colleen seemed to be the innocent in all this.

"We need to talk to Harold Bennison," Myrtle said, her cheeks flushed. "I want to hear what he has to say for himself."

I didn't disagree, but I didn't particularly feel like another visit to the golf estate. I was pretty sure Echo wouldn't be warmly received there.

"He likes an afternoon pie at The Spotted Spoon," Myrtle said, under her breath. "I've seen him there most afternoons."

"Really?" My ears pricked up, and I glanced at the clock on the wall.

"Yes. Why don't I stop by and I'll call you when he walks in."

"You'd do that?" It seemed I had a willing co-conspirator in the feisty librarian.

"Of course," she said with a firm nod. "I knew Harold when he was yay-high." She held her hand out at hip hight. "If he's been gambling, I'll have to have a strong word with him."

I smiled. I almost pitied Bennison.

Forty minutes later, I got a text message from Myrtle. "The eagle has landed..."

I chuckled. That obviously meant Bennison was at the diner.

Tapping Echo, I nodded to the door. "Let's go, buddy. We have an interrogation to conduct."

He was up like a shot, and I clipped on his lead. After hanging the half an hour sign—this might take longer than five minutes—we headed towards The Spotted Spoon.

I had to give Myrtle credit. She was sitting opposite Bennison, wagging her finger at him. He had a piece of apple pie in front of him but hadn't touched a bite. If there was anyone who could intimidate the wealthiest man in Cedar Hollow, it was his old school librarian.

Looked like Myrtle had done most of the work for me. I slid into the seat next to her, and said, "Hello, Mr. Bennison. Fancy seeing you here."

He grimaced sulkily. It really was quite amusing.

"Harold's been a naughty boy," Myrtle said, and I was immediately transported back to my high school days. She would have been a formidable woman back then.

Bennison flushed. "I'm a grown man, Myrtle. I can do as I choose."

"Not if it's illegal, you can't," she countered. "What will Felicity say?"

He paled. "You won't tell my wife, will you?"

"Not if you help us," I cut in.

Myrtle nodded, albeit reluctantly.

"What do you want to know?" He shifted in his seat.

"How long has the poker game been running?" I asked, before Myrtle could get another word in. As grateful as I was, I didn't want her monopolising the conversation.

Bennison thought for a moment. "I started going to Blade for my haircuts about six months ago, after he extended a personal invitation at one of the business association meetings. I was impressed by his confidence, and I'd heard good things. So I gave him a try."

I nodded, but I wasn't interested in Blade's legitimate business.

"When did he invite you to the poker game?"

"After my second appointment at his shop," Bennison answered. "We'd just finished up, and he dropped it into conversation. Asked if I was a betting man. I said I could be and he told me about the poker games. I had no idea he was hosting them underneath the store."

"The old speakeasy," Myrtle whispered.

He nodded. "We played every Wednesday night. Late. The game started at ten o'clock. Went on till about midnight, sometimes beyond."

A quiet evening of the week in a small, sleepy town. Not the time or place that law enforcement would suspect illegal activity.

"Did Blade keep any records of the winnings?" I wanted to know. There must be some way to prove what went on there, and who owed who money.

"He kept a leather-bound book with him. I assumed he used it to record the wins and losses at the end of night."

That was exactly what we needed. Unfortunately, I already knew the ledger wasn't at the barbershop. With the place now completely cleaned out, and the speakeasy forensically bare, it was long gone. If he had kept it there at all.

"Why did you leave Blade as a client and move over to Tank?" I asked.

Bennison shrugged. "It was silly, but I didn't want to spend too much time around Blade and make it easy for him to learn my tells. I was enjoying our weekly games, and I didn't want to lose too much. I took it so seriously that I even carried a deck of cards with me everywhere I went."

Myrtle tsked and gave him a disappointed look. He ignored her, but I could see it bothered him. I reached into my pocket and fished out the Ace of Spades Echo had found in the bunker. "Missing any?"

Bennison reached for it, surprised. "Yes. I'd wondered where that one had got to. Where'd you find it?"

"Echo found it in a bunker on your golf course."

He snorted. "Must have dropped it when I landed a ball in there last weekend."

"Did Blade ever confront you about leaving? I mean, he was obviously upset to lose you as a customer."

He shook his head. "No, he never said anything to me. I know he had a short fuse, but I made it clear I wasn't leaving the game, just the barbershop."

I nodded and glanced at Myrtle. Bennison wasn't involved. She gave me a little nod in agreement. Before we left, though, there was one more thing I wanted to ask him.

"Would you mind making a list of the others at the game? It would really help us figure out what happened to him."

He gasped. "You think one of the players killed him?"

"It's something the police will have to look into," I said. I could always pass the list over to Sheriff Annie, but I did want to see it first.

Myrtle slid a napkin and a pen from her purse across the table. Moving his pie aside, he scribbled down a few names.

I scanned the list, and my breath caught in my throat. One name stood out from the rest.

Suddenly, I knew who the murderer was.

Chapter 24

Spreading The Word

After I locked up that evening, I drove over to Will's workshop, hoping he'd still be there. As luck would have it, he was working late. I saw the light on in the back as I pulled up, and his truck still parked outside.

"Hello," I called, as Echo and I walked inside.

He came out from the back, dusting his hands on his jeans. His face still held the imprints of the mask that he'd just pulled off.

"Hey, Lucy. Good to see you."

I couldn't help but smile at his dishevelled state. With his hair all mussed and sawdust on his shirt, he looked kind of cute.

I held up the two beers and packet of chips I'd picked

up on the way over. "My turn," I said, setting them on the countertop.

"Ah, perfect. I could use a beer. Thanks."

He opened one and handed it to me, then opened the second for himself. Echo looked longingly at the bag of chips, but nobody offered him one. He had his supper waiting when we got home.

"Anything new to report?" Will asked, as he opened the bag and took a handful.

Echo started drooling.

"Heaps," I said, grinning. I told him what Bennison had said, and how Myrtle had strong-armed him into talking with us.

He laughed at that. "Typical. I'm glad he confirmed it though."

"He also gave us a list of players," I said, hesitantly. "You'll never guess who's on it."

I handed him the napkin, now a little crumpled.

His eyes ran down the names, and then his eyebrows shot up.

"Yeah, I know," I said.

He stared at me. "Have you spoken to the Sheriff?"

"Not yet. There's no evidence."

"It's her job to find the evidence," he pointed out. "You should take the list to her, Lucy."

"I know, and I will." I gnawed on my lower lip. "But I want to try something first."

He frowned. "I know I'm not going to like this."

Echo was looking at me like he was listening to every word I was saying, yet I knew he hadn't heard a thing. It was more likely the chip packet he was keeping an eye on.

"What if we make the killer think we have got evidence. Something that will prove they're the murderer?"

Will shook his head. "I'm not following."

"The 'little bird' network," I said, thinking of the past conversations I'd had with Myrtle. Will's face told me he didn't get that, either.

"A little birdie told me... You know how it is around here? News travels fast, whether you want it to or not."

That he understood.

"No kidding! I've heard things going around about me that I didn't even know myself."

"What if we take advantage of that?"

I started pacing, the movement kicking my brain into high gear.

"We spread the word around town about Blade's illegal poker den. We pretend it's all rumors at this point, that the sheriff's department still don't know about it. Maybe we say we're planning on telling Annie tomorrow."

Will nodded slowly. "You want to add in a few extra details?"

"Exactly." Now he was getting it. "We say there might be evidence down there. A ledger, containing all the names of the players. That'll make our suspect nervous. Really nervous."

Will raised his brows. "Nervous enough to make sure they get hold of the ledger before anybody else does."

I gave an excited nod. "We already know what they're capable of. Breaking into Blade's barbershop is going to be a cakewalk for our killer."

"And when they do," finished Will, "we'll be right there waiting for them."

I glanced down at Echo. Having given up on the chips, he'd laid down at my feet, but he wasn't asleep. He was watching me intently with his bright, golden-brown eyes.

I smiled. "And I know a very good boy who will definitely want to help."

Will and I spent a good hour hashing out the plans, before I took Echo home to feed him. It wasn't fair to eat all the chips and torture him, when I knew he must be hungry. Echo was always hungry.

The plan was simple, really. I'd meet Myrtle at The Spotted Spoon for coffee in the morning and tell her our scheme. From there on, she'd handle it.

"She's a natural," I'd told Will back at his workshop.

Will was going to speak to Junebug Harris, the mailman. A lifetime of delivering people's mail meant he knew most of the residents of Cedar Hollow. He would also help spread it around.

My final stop would be Curl Up & Dye for a chat with Dee.

And then we'd wait for the plan to unfold.

The next morning, Myrtle met me at the diner, as arranged. She was settled into her favorite spot by the front window, enjoying one of the diner's blueberry muffins when I arrived. She glanced up expectantly.

"I'm assuming you have some intel for me?" she whispered.

"Better than that," I replied, slipping into the seat across from her. "I have a plan, but I need your help."

I outlined my idea, and she nodded enthusiastically.

"Leave it with me," she said, breaking a large chunk out of her muffin and popping it into her mouth.

Will, I knew, was going to send a broken drill back to

the manufacturer for repair under warranty. I was impressed yet again. He'd come up with the perfect reason to stop by the post office and see Junebug without arousing any suspicion. That man was turning out to be as good at covert investigations as he was at carpentry.

I headed down the sidewalk with Echo to Dee's salon. My first idea had been to tell her I was there for more hair serum, but after a quick check of my bank balance, I decided I had already spent enough money on this case. My brand-new membership to the Cedar Ridge Golf Estate had cost me a fortune.

Instead, I went with updating her on Will's status as 'officially cleared' by the sheriff, which she probably already knew, but it was as good a reason as any. And I knew how she liked to talk about Will.

"I already heard," Dee told me pleasantly, breezing around her client with a bottle of hair spray. The skirt of her long-sleeved burgundy dress billowed behind her as she moved, and her chunky boots clunked against the floor.

"Close your eyes, honey," she instructed a brunette sitting in her chair with a fresh cut and blowout.

"Oh, I'm glad. How'd you hear?" I asked.

"Myrtle told a few of the girls from the mother's group at the diner, and I cut all their hair, so—" She shrugged.

The little bird network again. With a few long sprays, she released an artfully aimed fine mist. Echo, seated at my side, wrinkled his nose band sneezed.

"I know how relieved you must be," I added, with a teasing smile.

She shook her head. "It may come as a surprise to you, Lucy, but I've decided that Will's not my type."

"Oh?" This was news.

"I met a guy last weekend who actually likes me back."
She gave a self-deprecating grin. I decided I liked Dee.

"That's great," I said kindly.

She raised a perfectly shaped eyebrow. "I have noticed
Mr. Mercer paying *a lot* of little visits to your store lately,
however. Bringing you coffees, playing with your dog—"

She winked.

I laughed but knew I had to change the subject. Fast. I'd
come here to share gossip, not feature in it.

"We've been friends since I hired him to help me with
my renovations," I said quickly, "but he's also been helping
me look into Blade's murder."

"He has?"

"Yeah, and we found something. Something big."

Dee's eyes widened. "Ooh really? Tell me more."

In the mirror, Dee's client's gaze shifted upward to me.

I leaned forward, as if sharing a secret. "So listen to
this..."

Chapter 25

The Bust

Echo

We were getting close, I could feel it.

Rabbit had been acting different these last few days. Energized. Determined. She was working with Carpenter Man to track down suspects and interview them.

The evidence I'd found at the inn must have been a solid lead.

We'd been back to the first crime scene twice. Once to do a preliminary inspection, then to show the Police Officer.

Carpenter Man had been there, too. Gained entry for us. I noticed he hadn't used a key. As a trained K9 officer, I couldn't endorse illegal entry to private property. Not without a warrant.

Still, I knew how hard Rabbit had been hunting for

leads. Following up the evidence I found for her, too. I hoped this was the break she'd been looking for.

Carpenter Man was a constant surprise. He was learning. Getting smarter. Faster. His last situational awareness drill had been flawless. He'd intercepted me before I even got near the gloves.

I even awarded him bonus points for breaking into the barbershop without landing me or Rabbit in police lockup for trespassing. That would have been embarrassing.

Inside had been a shock, however. A lot had changed since the last time Rabbit and I had been there. That had been shortly after we'd first moved to town.

The upstairs was empty, like it had been completely cleaned out. I'd detected bleach, ammonia, and a bunch of other chemicals I couldn't name. They'd tickled my sensitive snout.

Downstairs was where we'd hit paydirt.

The place had been dusty, but what a find. A table and chairs, full of interesting scents. Sweat, fear, desperation.

The killer was on a few of them. I remembered the scent profile from the room that woman had died in, clear as day. They'd been there, relaxing, drinking, perspiring.

Rabbit had known it too, I could tell by the increase in her heartrate. This criminal's time was almost up.

The bust was happening tonight, I could sense it. My instinct was confirmed when, after closing, Rabbit put my lead on and we crept across the street to the barbershop. We snuck down the back alley, always a sure sign what we were doing wasn't supposed to be seen by anyone else.

Carpenter Man was waiting by the back door. I hoped he wasn't going to break in again. Much to my disappointment, he did, but Rabbit led me inside and I knew by her anxiety levels that she was relying on me to do a job.

I was ready.

It was dark inside, but that didn't bother me too much. I gave the upper level another cursory sniff. Nothing had changed since our last reconnaissance. No one else had been inside.

We went downstairs, and I did another sweep.

This time, they used their phones to light up the dark.

Again I found nothing and no one. Just dust, spiders, and the table in the middle of the room with the chairs. The scent profiles were still there, but fainter now.

Rabbit brought me back upstairs. To leave the premises, I assumed. But then she motioned to a back room.

Puzzled, I went to inspect it. It was some kind of storage space next to a bathroom. One small window, just big enough for the light from the street to shine through. There wasn't much there. Just a few toilet paper rolls and the smells of what had been in the room previously. Cardboard boxes. Plastic bottles and jars. Shaving foam and household disinfectant.

Everything smelled of the first vic. Big Burly Man. Made sense, since this was his shop.

There was no trace of the killer in here, so I turned to leave.

Instead of letting me out, Rabbit and Carpenter Man squeezed into the room with me. It was a tight fit, but they huddled together and closed the door.

What on earth—?

Something was going down, that much was clear. I stood to attention, waiting for orders.

Rabbit asked me to lie down, so I did.

Were we hiding? Was Rabbit afraid we were in danger?

I couldn't smell the right kind of visceral fear coming from her or from Carpenter Man, but I decided to make sure no one was approaching our location.

I crawled forward, through their legs, and pressed my nose to the gap under the door. Took a big sniff.

Rabbit touched me on the back of my neck, and I looked up at her. She signaled me to be quiet.

That's when I realized. We weren't *hiding* from someone. We were *waiting for* someone. This was a sting operation. We were lying in wait to catch the killer.

I settled against the floor, comfortable but ready. I took short, quick sniffs of the air, careful not to snort.

Rabbit wasn't afraid, but I could see that she was tense. Carpenter Man, too. Rabbit was making eye contact with me, but the look in her eyes was distant. She was listening. Waiting for a sound I wouldn't hear.

I kept my eyes on her and stayed calm. It was tough being patient during a sting, but that was the nature of covert police work. I knew this from experience. Torres and I had participated in plenty of undercover operations. Move too early and the whole thing was sunk. Months of good police work down the drain. I wasn't going to let that happen. Not to Rabbit. And not now, when life was finally getting interesting again.

Suddenly, Rabbit's expression changed. She'd heard something. She looked at Carpenter Man. He was frowning. Listening.

Sniff, sniff.

Yep, they were here. The killer was in the building.

I got to my paws, ready to move. Any minute now. Rabbit and Carpenter Man nodded to each other. Carefully, she reached for the doorknob, looked at me, and nodded.

She opened the door, and I went.

I couldn't see too well in the dark, so I followed my nose, my claws skittering and sliding across the floor. The door in the wall was ajar, the one that led to the basement. I head-butted my way through and bounded down the stairs.

The scent was getting stronger.

I burst into the cellar. The man was right there, in the middle of the room. I'd found him.

That's when I started barking.

Alert! Suspect detected!

The killer spun around, a look of fear on his face. Good.

Be afraid, perp. Be very afraid.

I leaped onto him, attempting to knock him to the ground. He stumbled, landing hard on his backside. He rolled and tried to throw me off.

Luckily for me—unluckily for him—I'd practiced apprehension scenarios like this a hundred times. Executed them a dozen times more.

I found the man's forearm, just like I'd been trained to do, and bit down.

He yowled, so loud even I could hear something.

Yell all you want, pal. You're not getting away.

Moments later, Rabbit and Carpenter Man burst onto the scene. The light flicked on, flooding the room. I was still battling with the killer, hanging on as he wrenched his arm back and forth.

I recognized him now. We'd met before. The other smells had been so strong that day, his hadn't stuck in my mind. But it did now.

Carpenter Man grabbed hold of the man, and Rabbit signaled for me to release my grip. I was so hyped, it took a few seconds for the command to sink in.

Release, she told me again. I opened my jaws and let go.

Carpenter Man hauled the killer to his feet.

Rabbit led me to the other side of the room but then crouched down and ruffled my ears. "Great job," I imagined her saying. This was confirmed when she pulled a handful of treats out of her pocket and fed them to me. Then she shot her hands into the air and wriggled her fingers.

Good boy! Good boy!

We'd done it. We'd finally caught the killer.

I looked over to where Carpenter Man had the suspect in a vice-like grip.

Time to face justice, Pancake Man.

Chapter 26

Never The One You Expect

Parker Dewey.

Thanks to Echo, we'd busted our murder suspect.

As I watched Will tighten his grip on Parker's arm, I couldn't help but think of the irony. The meekest, mildest-mannered man in Cedar Hollow—on the surface, at least—had turned out to be a cold-blooded killer.

Sheriff Annie was on her way, and Echo was on full alert, in case the suspect decided to make a break for it. With Will holding him in an armlock, I didn't think it likely.

Parker seemed to be in something of a daze. His customary polka-dot cravat was untucked and askew, and his cardigan hung open and was torn in a few places thanks to Echo's claws. He also gripped his arm where Echo's teeth had held him.

There was a strange look on his face, a combination of guilt and panic. His wide-eyed stare darted from Echo to me to the front door. I sensed his desire to bolt.

"The Sheriff won't be long," I told him, just in case he was getting any ideas.

"If you let me go," he blurted, his voice shrill, "I'll find a way to compensate you. Nobody else has to know about this. Be smart and let me pay you. I'll find a way to—"

"It's too late, Parker. Didn't you hear me? The Sheriff is on her way."

He trailed off as in the distance, sirens could be heard. A short time later, we heard the front door open, and foot-steps on the stairs.

Sheriff Annie appeared from the secret stairwell, but she wasn't alone. Reverend Heller was with her. I wasn't surprised to see Myrtle scurrying in behind them, bundled in her scarf. She looked excited, but also a little nervous.

"Myrtle, you can't be here," Annie announced, reaching for her cuffs.

"You got him!" Myrtle exclaimed, her gaze drifting to Parker. Annie threw up her hands in exasperation.

Annie threw up her hands. "Doesn't anyone listen to me anymore?"

The cuffs snapped on and Parker groaned, as he realized he was indeed caught.

I could see why the reverend was there. As a trusted figure in town, Sheriff Annie had probably asked him to come along, hoping he'd help Parker relax enough to tell the truth. He was carrying a red bag marked with a thick white cross—the first aid box I'd requested for the dog bite.

The reverend pulled out a chair from beneath the poker table. "Have a seat," he said to Parker. Reluctantly, Parker lowered himself into it and placed his cuffed hands on the table.

Will pulled out chairs for me, Sheriff Annie, Myrtle and himself. He arranged them in a semicircle around Parker and The Boss. Now it felt less like an interrogation and more of a community intervention.

It had taken some convincing, but Annie had agreed to go along with it when I'd called her. I'd explained that I hoped it would be enough to get Parker to open up. Because what evidence did we really have? He wasn't on any camera footage. His DNA wasn't found at any crime scene—yet. We didn't have the ledger.

Apart from his name on a napkin and the fact he'd broken into the barbershop, we had nothing. Certainly not enough to convict.

If I'd brought my suspicions and a shiny black button to my editor at the paper, much less the district attorney who would decide whether to go to trial, I would have been laughed out of the newsroom.

We needed a confession.

"Mind if I take a look at your arm?" Reverend Heller asked.

Parker gave a grateful nod. The reverend gingerly pulled up the sleeve of his cardigan. Echo's teeth had broken the skin, but it wasn't a bad bite.

"Can you wiggle your fingers?" the reverend asked.

Parker nodded, and did so, casting a scathing look at Echo.

Opening his first aid bag, the reverend pulled out a pair of clean latex gloves, a bottle of disinfectant, gauze, and bandage tape. Quietly, he got to work.

"Why don't you tell us what you're doing here, Parker?" Annie asked, taking out her notebook.

"Am I under arrest?" he asked.

"No, you're being given a chance to explain yourself. If you try to leave, I will arrest you and we can do this down at the station in an interrogation room."

I suppressed a grin. There were no flies on Annie.

Parker sighed and stared at the faded linoleum floor but didn't speak.

I glanced at Annie. "Mind if I say something?"

She gestured for me to go ahead.

I looked at Parker. "I think I know what happened here," I began. "How about I tell the story, and you let me know if I'm right?"

Parker's eyes burned into mine. "Go ahead," he said. "I'll just deny everything."

He probably would—at first. I expected him to. But every man had a breaking point. I was determined to find his.

"Blade was running an illegal poker game," I began. "Down here, out of his grandfather's old speakeasy. It was a good way to make money, until it wasn't. I think Blade got himself in a little too deep."

Parker's eyebrows went up, but he didn't say anything.

"On the day he was murdered," I went on, "Blade got into an argument with Tank Delgado at my store. He was angry that one of his clients, Harold Bennison, had switched over to Tank's barbershop. It didn't make a lot of sense to me at the time, but it does now. Blade was having money trouble. He had a debt to Will for renovation work that he couldn't pay. Gambling debts, too, probably, that were sinking him. Sinking him so badly that he'd resorted to selling his shop. And until that deal was done, losing a wealthy client like Bennison was a blow to his bottom line. A blow he couldn't afford."

Parker's gaze didn't budge from my face. "What does this have to do with me?"

"A lot," I said. "Because Bennison wasn't just a client of Blade's, he was a player in his poker game. But you'd know that, because you were, too."

I paused to see if Parker would respond. He didn't. I kept going anyway. I had a few more details to share before it would be time to pull him back into the story.

"Even though Bennison switched barbers, he had every intention of sticking with the poker game," I went on. "He went over to Tank because he didn't want Blade to figure out his tells. But, to Blade, losing Bennison as a client was a big risk. It might mean Bennison was planning to talk, planning to out him to the sheriff. So Blade was more than a little on edge the night he was killed. That's why he argued with Tank. And it's why he argued with Will, too, about the bill he owed from when Will renovated his shop."

In my peripheral vision, I could see Myrtle hanging on my every word. Sheriff Annie was also listening intently, while Will nodded along. Reverend Heller had a fixed, stunned look on his face, as though he hadn't realized what he was walking into when he agreed to accompany the sheriff to the barbershop tonight.

I'd spent most of my career figuring out complex crimes and scandals and telling their stories. I was made for this.

"Will left by the back door of the barbershop that night," Myrtle cut in, suddenly eager to contribute. "Was that because of the argument?"

"Yes. He was in a hurry to get out of there after they had words," I said, with a glance at Will. Dee's dignity would be preserved. "But he wasn't the only one who used the back door that night. Parker, here, snuck in through the back, killed Blade with his own razor, then got out without being seen. It took him just under ten minutes, because that's all the time he had."

Parker shot me a sharp look. He finally had something to say.

"It's impossible to do all that in ten minutes," he scoffed. "Anyway, I was having dinner that night with Colleen, at the Inn. Multiple people can confirm that, including my wife, who knew my plans. The waitress, too."

The time had come.

"You're right," I agreed. "You were having dinner with Colleen at the restaurant at the Inn, and multiple people did see you there, including the waitress. But, she didn't have eyes on you the whole time."

"What do you mean? I was right there at the table."

"Bathroom breaks," I said. "You took one when Colleen stepped outside to talk to her daughter who'd called from France. But you skipped the restroom and snuck out the back of the restaurant, crossed Main Street down the block to avoid the front door camera, zigzagged through a few backyards to get to Spurlock Road. From there, you ran into the alley behind that whole block of stores, right to the barbershop."

Parker's eyelids flickered. "You think I'm that fast? I'd have to be an athlete to make it there and back in the time you're suggesting."

"Well, no. It's not that far," Myrtle piped up. "It can't be more than a quarter of a mile each way. Even I could do that, and you're a good few decades younger than me, Parker Dewy."

Myrtle leaned forward, her eyes sharp. "Weren't you training for a half marathon? Your wife told me all about it the other day. She said you'd given up smoking, too, even though she caught you with a pack at the pancake breakfast."

I gazed over at him triumphantly. Myrtle had done it again.

"It was a 5K," Parker corrected, bleakly. "A fun run."

"So you're actually quite fit," I concluded, sending Myrtle a grateful nod. "Aren't you?"

Parker deflected. "Even if I were, why would I go to all that trouble to get to Blade's shop? I could have stopped by to see him anytime."

"You wanted to get him alone," I pointed out. "It was after closing, but you knew he would still be there, getting ready for poker night. You wanted to give him one last chance to forgive your debt."

"My debt?"

"Your gambling debt," I stated. "The one you couldn't pay. The one you were hiding from your wife. That's the thing with problem gambling. It can catch up with you—fast."

"How do you—?" he stammered, white as a sheet.

Then a resigned look came into his eyes.

"You found the ledger, didn't you?"

I glanced at Annie, then nodded. He didn't need to know we had no idea where the ledger was. If that's what it took to get him to confess...

He shook his head, his words bitter. "Do you know how it feels when you realize you've risked your family's financial future—and lost? When there's no way out? My wife would have never forgiven me if she knew the trouble we were in. The trouble I got us into."

Reverend Heller put a hand on Parker's shoulder. "I know you didn't mean for things to get so out of control," he said kindly.

Parker blinked back tears. "I tried to stay away, but Blade kept pressuring me to come back. I was making him a lot of money, I guess. On paper, anyway. I couldn't pay him. Not unless I sold my house. Cancelled my daughter's college tuition. Ruined our retirement. It was a nightmare."

"So you tried to talk to Blade," I offered. "You tried to reason with him one last time."

"No." Parker fixed me with an empty stare. "That's where you're wrong. There was no reasoning with him."

"So you murdered him," I whispered.

Parker looked around the group, pleading with us to understand. "I had to make it right for my family. I had to find my own way out."

A grim understanding settled over the room. With Blade gone, Parker's debt would be erased.

Sheriff Annie cleared her throat. "Am I to understand, you came here with the intent to kill Blade Cavanaugh?"

Parker's response was a soft moan. "Yes."

There was a moment of silence, where nobody said anything.

"What about Colleen?" I whispered, recovering first. "Why did you strangle her?"

"It wasn't intentional," he said. "I was pleased to see Colleen. We were old friends."

"Friends don't murder each other," Myrtle remarked, her arms crossed.

"Was it because she'd seen you?" I asked.

He shook his head. "No, she didn't see me."

"Then why?" Annie asked. I was surprised to find my theory had been incorrect.

Parker shook his head, dejected. He had nothing to lose, now. He was already going away for life.

"Blade was dead, but the nightmare wasn't over. I knew

he'd kept a ledger. A record of our losses. It was only a matter of time before someone found it, and then the whole thing would come out."

He snorted as if to say, like this.

"I asked Colleen for a favor."

I suddenly clicked.

"You asked her to break into Blade's shop and get it for you." The night Echo and I had stopped Colleen from breaking into Blade's shop, she *had* been after his books. Just not the accounts.

"I told her I'd left something in there, a private ledger from the Historical Society's collection, and she agreed to get it for me. Except she couldn't gain access. It was only later, when I asked her to go back, that she demanded to know what I was really after."

"You told her about the gambling," I guessed. "You opened up so she would help you, but instead she put two and two together. Did she figure out it was you who'd killed Blade?"

Parker nodded. "She stopped answering my texts. I went by the inn to see her, the night before she was due to leave. I begged for her help. She was supposed to be my friend." His face crumpled. "She said she wouldn't protect me. That she was going to call the sheriff. I had to stop her."

I glanced at Annie. That's why Colleen had dialed the sheriff's office.

"So you killed her," Annie said quietly, her face drawn. "You attacked her and strangled her to stop her making that call."

Peter gave a sullen nod.

It was then that I noticed the black buttons on his cardigan. A few were hanging loose, held only by a thread. But one, at the very top, was missing.

I glanced down at Echo. He sat beside my chair, not taking his eyes off Parker. Somehow, he had figured out that button was important. Whether by smell or pure instinct, I had no idea. But he'd brought it right to me.

I felt a lump rise in my throat.

Echo really was special. Despite what we'd each been through, and after all the big changes and challenges of moving to Cedar Hollow, we were a team now. A good one.

Parker sat slumped in his chair, hands cuffed in front of him. All the fight had left his body, and he looked like a hollow shell of a man.

Sheriff Annie stood up.

"Parker Dewey," she said. "You're under arrest for the murders of Blade Cavanaugh and Colleen Cavanaugh."

Myrtle's Apple Pie And A Date

It was official. Myrtle's apple pie was better than what they served at the Cedar Hollow Inn restaurant.

At Sheriff Annie's invitation, a few of us gathered for a celebration after hours at the sheriff's station. It had been a few days since Parker's arrest. The double murderer was long gone, shipped off to the county jail to await trial.

It had been an emotional week for the citizens of Cedar Hollow. Parker's wife was understandably devastated. The community was in shock. Nobody, me included, had suspected the meek, mild-mannered historian capable of murder.

Despite the heaviness that hung over the town in the aftermath of Parker's arrest, Sheriff Annie wouldn't let us skip the celebration. I guess it was her way of trying to raise our spirits.

When Echo and I walked into the conference room at the sheriff's office, I was surprised and a little embarrassed to be greeted by a chorus of whoops and cheers from Dee, Reverend Heller, Myrtle, and of course, Will. Only Annie and her deputies didn't chime in.

"We're just so proud of you, dear," exclaimed a beaming Myrtle. She rummaged in her tote and pulled out a packet of Yummy Nummy dog treats that I'd sold her the day before.

Cheddar cheese flavor.

She tossed it into the air and Echo caught it with a succinct *chomp*. Everybody clapped again.

"What a good boy!" Myrtle exclaimed. "We're very proud of you, too, Echo!"

Annie walked over, hand extended. "Lucy, congratulations. It pains me to say it, but I'm not sure if we'd have caught him if it wasn't for you."

I laughed as I shook it. "It wasn't just me. It was all of us."

The 16-seater table was covered in snacks and desserts. It seemed everybody had contributed. There was Myrtle's apple pie, Dee's fancy cheese platter with crackers, the reverend had bought chips and dip, and Will had brought a plate of homemade sandwiches. They were good, too: some roast beef, others cucumber and cream cheese, plus a spicy egg salad that had The Boss going back for more.

Did the man's talents never end?

"Was it Parker's name on the list that did it?" Myrtle asked me, once we had all loaded up our paper plates and found a place to sit. Dee and Sheriff Annie had branched off into their own conversation, while in the background, I could hear Reverend Heller telling the deputies about the latest Springsteen concert he'd been to.

Echo sat right next to my chair, his eyes ever hopeful. Will came over to join us.

I nodded, my mouth full. Once I'd swallowed, I said, "That's when it all fell into place. If Parker was a gambler, he could have owed money. He was one of the few people Colleen knew in town. She told me that herself. Who else would she have opened her hotel door to? Invited in to her room?"

Myrtle nodded, while Will studied me with something like pride in his eyes.

"There were a few other things," I continued, not wanting to think about what that meant right now. "At the pancake breakfast, Echo knocked over a tin of petty cash, and there was a poker chip in there. I barely noticed it because of all the fuss about the cigarettes. But it made sense after I'd seen that list of names."

"He sure had a lot of secrets, didn't he?" tsked Myrtle.

"I knew I liked you the moment I met you," Myrtle said, raising her glass to me. "Lucy, you're a wonderful addition to our little community, and we're lucky to have you."

"Hear-hear," echoed Will, softly.

"I'm glad to be here, too," I croaked out, feeling emotional. "Echo feels the same way, don't you, old man?" I stroked his fur so they wouldn't see the tears that had sprung into my eyes, and my dog glanced up. I could have sworn he gave a nod.

For the first time since we'd arrived in Cedar Hollow, I felt like I belonged. These people were my friends, my community. It was a heady feeling.

"Everybody, I'd like to say a few words," Sheriff Annie announced, saving me from turning into a blubbering mess.

She stood at the end of the table holding a plastic cup of sparkling juice. "I want to thank you all for the part you played in solving the murders of Blade and Colleen Cavanaugh. It's inspiring to live and work in a community that cares so much about its citizens."

There was a smattering of applause.

But Annie wasn't done.

"And I want to take this opportunity to recognize someone who played a huge part in this investigation. Brave, selfless, and heroic, this individual never backed down from danger. We were all kept safer by their actions, and I, for one, am deeply grateful for their help." She looked at my dog. "Echo, come on up here."

I touched the back of his neck and asked him to stand. The sheriff held out a handful of dog treats, courtesy of Myrtle.

Echo trotted up to her and executed a perfect sit.

"On behalf of the Cedar Hollow Sheriff's Department, I hereby bestow Echo Hart with his own honorary Cedar Hollow Deputy's badge." She reached into her back pocket and pulled out a shiny plastic police badge, which she clipped to his collar.

I grinned and joined everyone in a round of applause.

Later, as we were preparing to leave, Annie came over to me and Echo. She glanced fondly down at him.

"I know your secret," she said.

I tensed. Had she figured out my dog was deaf?

Or that I was developing a pretty big crush on Will?

She gestured to Echo, and I felt myself relax. "I'd have

to be blind not to recognize a fellow law enforcement officer."

Busted.

"He's retired," I said quickly.

Annie gave a little laugh. "We never retire. It's in the blood."

I smiled at that.

"The thing is, I'd rather you kept that to yourself. You see, Echo helped bring down a lot of bad people, people he can identify. If they knew he was alive—" I faded off, not wanting to think about what that meant.

"I understand," she said, sagely. "His secret is safe with me."

"Thank you."

Will caught my eye from across the room. The corners of his mouth edged up into that slow smile.

I returned it. *Definitely cute.*

"Got any plans for the weekend?" he asked, walking me out.

"I might take a long walk with Echo," I said. "Drive south and check out the last of the leaves before they all fall."

"I know a few good walking trails down that way," he suggested. "Some nice old, covered bridges, too. Not sure if you've visited any of them yet."

"I haven't explored much beyond Cedar Hollow," I admitted. The last six months had been all about getting the store ready to sell, and then when we stayed, I'd been adjusting to our new routine.

"I'd be happy to take you myself, if you like. I've got plenty of room in my pickup for both of you."

Will's brown eyes were warm and sincere. This time, I didn't feel my cheeks turning pink. Instead, my stomach did a little flip. In a good way. The kind that made you want to say yes.

"I would love to," I said.

Will grinned. "So, it's a date?"

"Definitely." I grinned back. "It's a date."

Ready for another mystery to solve? Click here to pre-order book two, *Old Tricks, New Trouble*, or by using the link below!
https://a.co/d/ogNkR7Ce

Did you enjoy *The Barbershop Showdown*? Don't forget to leave a review to let us know your thoughts!
https://a.co/d/f8afl17

Canine Confidential Series

The Barbershop Showdown

Old Tricks, New Trouble

Also by Ellie Webster

Tails of Maple Ridge

The Peanut Butter Twist

Paws and Prejudice

Canine Confidential

The Barbershop Showdown

Old Tricks, New Trouble

Tangled Threads Mysteries

The Deadly Tapestry

Don't miss out on exclusive cozy content— sign up for the Ellie Webster newsletter today!

https://www.getdrip.com/forms/99805461/submissions/new

About the Author

Ellie Webster is the shared pen name for a small group of writers who adore all things cozy and mysterious. Set in the picturesque towns of New England, Ellie's stories feature lovable amateur sleuths, loyal pets, and plenty of twists tucked between cups of coffee and community gossip. Expect warmth, wit, and a mystery that keeps you turning the pages long after lights-out.

Perfect for readers who enjoy a steaming mug beside them, a faithful cat or dog at their feet, and the comforting promise that justice (and a slice of pie) will always be served.

instagram.com/authorelliewebster

tiktok.com/@authorelliewebster

www.ingramcontent.com/pod-product-compliance
Lightning Source LLC
Chambersburg PA
CBHW032011050726
47590CB00006B/2129